GennaRose Nethercott

FIFTY BEASTS TO BREAK YOUR HEART

GennaRose Nethercott is a writer and folklorist. She is the author of a novel, *Thistlefoot*. Her first book, *The Lumberjack's Dove*, was selected by Louise Glück as a winner of the National Poetry Series, and whether authoring novels, poems, ballads, or even fold-up paper cootie catchers, her projects are all rooted in myth—and what our stories reveal about who we are. She tours widely, performing strange tales (sometimes with puppets in tow), and helps create the podcast *Lore*. She lives in the woodlands of Vermont, beside an old cemetery.

FIFTY
BEASTS
TO BREAK
YOUR HEART

FIFTY
BEASTS
to BREAK
your HEART

& OTHER STORIES

GennaRose Nethercott

VINTAGE BOOKS
A Division of Penguin Random House LLC
New York

A VINTAGE BOOKS ORIGINAL 2024

Portions of this work have previously appeared in the following publications:
"A Diviner's Abecedarian" in *The American Scholar*; "Sundown at the Eternal
Staircase" in *BOMB* magazine; "Drowning Lessons" in *The Literary Review*;
an early flash-fiction version of "The Autumn Kill" in *Wyvern Lit*; "The Autumn
Kill" in *The Massachusetts Review* (print only); excerpts from "Fifty Beasts to Break
Your Heart" in *The Spectacle*, *BOMB* magazine, *TIMBER*, *The Massachusetts Review*,
Phantom Drift, and *Tilted House*.

Library of Congress Cataloging-in-Publication Data
Names: Nethercott, GennaRose, author.
Title: Fifty beasts to break your heart : & other stories / by GennaRose Nethercott.
Description: First edition. | New York : Vintage Books, a division of Penguin
Random House LLC, 2024.
Identifiers: LCCN 2023017473 (print) | LCCN 2023017474 (ebook)
Subjects: LCGFT: Fantasy fiction. | Fairy tales. | Short stories.
Classification: LCC PS3614.E5229 F54 2024 (print) | LCC PS3614.E5229 (ebook) |
DDC 813/.6—dc23
LC record available at https://lccn.loc.gov/2023017473
LC ebook record available at https://lccn.loc.gov/2023017474

Vintage Books Trade Paperback ISBN: 978-0-593-31418-0
eBook ISBN: 978-0-593-31419-7

Book design by Christopher M. Zucker

vintagebooks.com

Printed in the United States of America
10 9 8 7 6 5 4 3 2 1

To the Autumn People.
Blessed Be the Bones!

CONTENTS

FIFTY
BEASTS
TO BREAK
YOUR HEART

SUNDOWN AT THE ETERNAL STAIRCASE

Do not enter the Eternal Staircase after 8 p.m.

No outside food or drink is permitted within the Eternal Staircase.

Black-soled sneakers, high-heeled shoes, and flip-flops are prohibited inside the Eternal Staircase.

No dogs.
    (Yes, we used to allow dogs. Too many dogs shit in the Eternal Staircase.)

If you feel light-headed within the Eternal Staircase, alert a staff member immediately. Eternal Staircase staff can be identified by their blue polo shirts, blue visors, and our official WATCH YOUR STEP! lapel pins.

(Do not engage with staff members without official lapel pins. They are likely a Disgraced staff member. Disgraced staff members spent too much time in the Eternal Staircase and were asked to leave. They keep returning anyway. We don't know how to get rid of them. They are not helpful.)

Absolutely NO RUNNING down into the Eternal Staircase. Running in the Eternal Staircase is a criminal offense and punishable by law.

Do not remain in the Eternal Staircase for more than three consecutive hours.

Do not descend deeper than the yellow ribbons marked GO BACK!

Welcome to the Eternal Staircase, and remember— Watch Your Step!

∽

June worked the afternoon shift. Harebell worked the midnight shift. Their shifts overlapped for three hours at sunset. Sunset was a busy time at the Eternal Staircase and required extra staff. The lilac and coral and opal of the sky would reflect off the blue tiles shelling the stairs, causing the spectacle to melt with dark, multicolored light. Sunset was also when visitors were most likely to trip on the Eternal Staircase, and when the most trash was dropped, and when June and Harebell could most easily vanish into the crowd to drink brandy from Harebell's flask behind the hotdog stand.

∽

"Would you rather have eyelashes for teeth or have to work here forever?"

"Could I pluck the eyelashes out or put dentures over them?"

"No."

"Would other people in the world have eyelash teeth? Would there be a community of eyelash-teeth havers?"

"No. You'd be the only person ever born with eyelash teeth."

"I'd still go for that."

"There's no guarantee things are any better at other jobs."

"I know."

Harebell scratched her ear with a bobby pin, then used it to clip back a chunk of powder-pink hair. Twenty feet away, a kid dropped a plastic guzzler cup, spilling neon slushy down the Eternal Staircase.

"Ah, fuck," said June, jumping up.

Harebell kissed two fingers and held them to the sky. "An offering to the deep!"

June pulled a rag from the staff kit in her fanny pack and headed toward the spill. Harebell didn't move to help.

∽

The Eternal Staircase contains an undetermined number of blue granite steps, arranged in a circular well, roughly the circumference of a football field. Every individual navy stair is slicked with a mosaic of 1,424 small blue tiles, each the size of a fingernail. The well grows narrower the deeper you descend. Mathematicians claim that the Eternal Staircase's gradual narrowing must be an optical illusion, as the Eternal Staircase never seems to fully taper off. No one has ever reached the bottom of the Eternal Staircase. There may or may not be a bottom to the Eternal Staircase, but if there is one, the Eternal Staircase certainly does not want anyone to know.

～

No one worked at the Staircase for more than a summer. Well, almost no one. Weird things happened to people who stayed too long. Ennui. Bouts of dizziness. Violent dreams. Dreams about animals with multiple heads or no heads at all. Suspicious numbers of molar cavities. There were all sorts of urban legends about the Eternal Staircase. Where it came from. Where it led. What it could do to you if you weren't careful. June and Harebell thought it was bullshit. Maybe the weird dreams thing was true, but beyond that, everyone quit by September because it was just a gross place to work.

Charlie, the manager, wore the same paisley button-down every day and called all women "Sweetie" instead of their names. He owned a plot of land out west that he claimed was a genuine gold mine (he had yet to find a single flake of gold), and he was always making people look at photos of the acreage on his phone. Charlie paid minimum wage and not a cent more, and only hired girls he thought were hot. Half the time the paychecks bounced, and he had to wait until the hotdog stand had enough money to pay the employees from the register.

Then there was the work itself: huffing up and down the Staircase, mopping up ketchup and Cheeto spills, getting yelled at by road-tripping tourists who threatened to sue after stubbing a sandaled toe on a stone step. It could have been labeled "character building" if it weren't so sleazy.

Harebell was the exception to the summer rule. While June had been there only since school let out, Harebell had worked there a year and a half.

"It's temporary, though," she insisted, rolling a joint in the shadow of the hotdog stand. She licked the paper edge, sealed it shut. "I'm gonna move to Portland, open a tattoo shop. I bought a tattoo gun online, been practicing on grapefruits. I'll do one on you if you want."

"Yeah?" June said. "What should I get?"

"Whatever you want, baby. Whatever you want. I have to practice—then, when I'm good enough, I'm out of here."

Peanut Dave popped his head out of the hotdog stand. "Can I get one?"

When he wasn't slinging concessions, Peanut Dave drove a van with GUINNESS WORLD RECORD PEANUT BUTTER EATER, 1992 painted on the side. There was a slot cut into the van where people could leave donations. Charlie strictly forbade this solicitation—but if you want an autograph, just ask and Peanut Dave will provide.

"Sure, D. But I get to choose what you're getting. And you can't look till I'm done."

"Skin's skin," he said. "We're all gonna rot one day anyway. Draw a dick on me, I don't care."

"Give him a peanut," June said. "Or a hotdog."

"A little something to remember me by before I go."
Harebell winked at him.

～

There was a small casino on the south side of town and
a gaggle of small art galleries feathering Main Street, but
nothing measured up to the Eternal Staircase. Most of
the town's economy relied on tourists trickling off the
highway to gawk at the spiral of tiled steps, which gaped
like an animal's maw. It was the town's pride and its curse.
While the residents relied on the Eternal Staircase for
financial security, they had to spend their lives pretend-
ing to care about it. There were shops selling postcards of
the Staircase, little shot glasses with the Staircase etched
into the side, key chains that read WATCH YOUR STEP!
Even the high school mascot was a single rectangular
navy stair named Trip—a poor rival for the neighboring
town's Killer the Whale. The Eternal Staircase seemed to
cast a blue haze over the whole region, and you couldn't
get out from under it until you crossed the county line.

June and Harebell had lived near the Staircase their
whole lives. They had dozens of friends who'd quit jobs
at the Eternal Staircase and left for the city. Most boo-
meranged back. People raised near the Eternal Staircase
had a hard time adjusting to life without it. Townies
hated the Staircase, but whenever they went too far they
felt like something was missing. The land elsewhere
made too much sense. There was nothing to fall down
and keep falling.

～

There were two ways to tell what Harebell was thinking. First: ask her. Second, if the first didn't work (it rarely did): check her hair. Harebell had developed a complex and deliberate visual code based on the Danger Babe semi-permanent hair dye catalog. If she was happy or flirty, her hair was Cotton Candy Pink. If she was restless: Lemonade Ice Pop. On Stoplight Red days, she'd yell at you without provocation and steal lawn ornaments from strangers' houses to sell on eBay. Blizzard Blue was when she was horniest, though it could also mean she'd overslept, or just binged a good TV show. Slime-Time Green days were suspiciously friendly, with a monkey's paw generosity. Those days never ended well. One Slime-Time Green incident involved Harebell inviting the whole Staircase staff out to dinner, only to vanish from the falafel shop when the bill arrived. She didn't apologize—frankly, she thought they should have taken one look at her and known better. Anyone who couldn't predict Harebell's future actions based on her past cosmetic choices simply wasn't paying attention and deserved whatever was coming.

∽

Activities at the Eternal Staircase:
- Slinky launches begin at the Exhibit Banister every 45 minutes.
- Staircase aerobics classes are held twice daily, at 2 p.m. and 4 p.m.
- Lectures on the Eternal Staircase's history and design are on the third Thursday of every month.
  (Nothing is known about the history of the Eternal Staircase prior to its purchase by

the current owners in 1989. Do not attend the lecture if you plan to ask any questions we cannot answer.)

Visitors who experience the sudden urge to descend deep into the Eternal Staircase—very deep, deeper than our staff can follow—must vacate the attraction immediately. Return to your car. Drive far away. Do not stop, even for tolls. Go home.

∾

"I've been working on something."

Harebell dropped a backpack with a broken zipper into June's lap. The opening was tacked shut with a dozen safety pins, which she left June to unclip, one by one. Inside the bag was a baby. That's what June thought at first anyway. She took it out, turned it around in her hands. It was a lump of clay the size of a basketball. Still soft. And it was human, in some ways—it had a face, certainly, with a button nose and dopey eyes. But it also had four stub horns poking out of its forehead, and the beginnings of dark, squishy wings.

"It's a demon kid," said Harebell.

"Yeah. I got that." June covered its face with the bag.

"Cool, right? I've been getting into sculpture. Thought I could leave it on a doorstep somewhere uptown. Spook some yuppies on their way to work in the morning."

"Maybe they'd adopt it," June said. "Raise it as their own."

"You know where I got the clay, though?" Harebell lifted an eyebrow and slid her mouth to the left of her face. It was a look June had come to recognize, for the sake of survival more than intimacy. It meant Harebell was up to some real weird shit.

"...Where?"

Harebell pointed down into the Eternal Staircase. June knew what she meant—she meant *deep* in the Staircase. Past the park limits. Into parts of the Staircase that would get you Disgraced immediately if Charlie knew you'd gone down there.

"Hare, don't get yourself fired. If I have to spend all day hanging out with Peanut Dave instead of you I'll throw myself down the stairs."

"But look, it's so cute!" Harebell uncovered the clay baby and nuzzled her nose against its clay nose. A dot of red earth smeared off on her. She wiped it on June.

The trouble had started a week earlier. Harebell was short on rent. She started taking on doubles. The normal six-hour shifts already spanned twice the doctor-recommended length of time to spend in the Eternal Staircase, and now Harebell was there twelve hours a day at least three times a week. She started slipping up. Forgetting to take her birth control pill. Leaving bleach in her hair too long on Lunar Platinum days. Missing appointments. But it wasn't like Harebell worked hard. She always shrugged the real dirty work onto whoever else was around. Now she had twice the time for workplace neglect. She was bored. She started wandering deeper and deeper into the Eternal Staircase to pass the time. Started bringing artifacts back up with her—shards of pottery, a fistful of metal guitar strings, a gold-plated pocket mirror. Things that had been lost to the Staircase years, maybe decades, before. Sometimes, bones. Her broken backpack grew heavy with junk, rattling like a tambourine as she moved up and down the stairs. Whenever she returned from below, her pupils were stretched so wide, the whole of her eyes were black. Obsidian orbs.

"What's even down there that's so worth it?" asked June.

"Nothing," said Harebell. "I mean, actual nothing. Can you imagine? Nothing that goes on forever . . ."

"There's got to be a bottom eventually," June said.

"Does there?" asked Harebell.

⟳

Once, June saw a man fall on the Eternal Staircase and snap a leg so clean that the bone folded in half as if there were an extra knee. When she touched the leg, it was rubbery and warm like a hot-water bottle. The man refused to be carried out until he had watched the sunset. Charlie gave the man a lifetime visitor's pass to the Eternal Staircase. June hoped he would never come back.

⟳

Visitors: Note the four large clocks posted around the perimeter of the Eternal Staircase. Please check regularly to avoid overstaying the three-hour recommended visitation limit.

Sometimes, what feels like five minutes within the Eternal Staircase is actually hours. Sometimes, what feels like hours is actually many, many days. Before we installed the clocks, there was no way to tell if you had been in the Eternal Staircase for an afternoon or multiple years. The Eternal Staircase is just that fun!

～

Some people think the Eternal Staircase leads down to hell. Officially, this has been neither confirmed nor denied.

～

The sun dipped down early. Harebell's hair was Violet Riot. She had stolen a book on the history of leopard print and given it to June. June loved leopard print. Harebell hated leopard print. She hated a lot of things that June liked: Paul Simon, the word *fizzy*, bananas, the banjo. But she didn't fully hate June. And June didn't hate the taste of brandy on Harebell's mouth as she leaned in and kissed her. Sweet and smoky. She hooked her tongue around Harebell's, and Harebell giggled into June's teeth. Beneath the liquor was something else, another flavor. A taste like earth, like clay. Like something buried, or unburied. Across the Eternal Staircase, the neon of the entry gate flickered, "Watch Your Step!"

～

Once, a guest fell in love with one of the glossy steps. He visited the step every day. He brought flowers to the step, adorning it in roses and baby's breath and pink tulips. He scattered small offerings across the step— metal charms and chocolates and silk ribbons tied into plump bows. He would lay on the step for hours each afternoon, whispering to it. The keepers of the Eternal Staircase let him be. Maybe they had looser rules back then. Maybe they found the man charming. Maybe they wanted to know why this one step was any different from the endless others. It went on like this for a time, and all was well. But then one day, the man arrived at the Eternal Staircase only to find that during the night, the staff had cleared away his flowers and talismans and gifts. The man couldn't tell which step was his step. They say the man wandered the Eternal Staircase for weeks, for months, searching for his step. They say he crawled the Staircase on his hands and knees until they bled. He never found his love. Or if he did, he passed right over it without recognition. They all looked the same.

～

We're trying to tell you that this has all happened before.

～

You go up the stairs and go down the stairs. You pay ten dollars for a metal slinky and watch it somersault forever. You've been to the Grand Canyon, the White Sands National Park, the Statue of Liberty. You've seen the world's largest pistachio at a truck stop in New Mexico. Here, you ask a stranger to take your picture sitting on the steps. The next day, driving down I-95, you reach into your jacket pocket for the blue tile you bought at the gift shop. Your reflection fumbles for space in the tiny square as you journey onward, away from the Eternal Staircase and the town that carries it. Farther, toward something new.

～

If you're wondering whether June was in love with Harebell, it's safe to say she wasn't *not* in love with her. That is, she'd bought at least two pairs of combat boots to impress Harebell, and those things aren't cheap, so you can draw your own conclusion.

Once, June had a dream that Harebell had a forked tongue. In the dream, they were making out until June realized that the left half of Harebell's tongue had gotten bored and ditched her for the arcade. June was so embarrassed that she started crying, and the tears were all little tongues, wriggling down her cheeks like leeches. If quantity of tongues equals severity of love, then June might have had a problem.

Was Harebell in love with June? No. Harebell was only in love with herself. And the Ramones. And maybe the Eternal Staircase.

❦

Visitors, this is not the kind of story we would tell you if it were unimportant. Luckily, it contains numerous incredibly important elements:

1) Two girls kissing behind a hotdog stand
2) An abyss
3) A sketchy roadside attraction by the highway
4) A decision that may not be a decision at all

Every one of these is important enough to merit us telling you. Imagine if we did not tell you about the WATCH YOUR STEP! key chains, where would you be then? Imagine if we failed to warn you that sometimes, decisions are made for us. That sometimes, staircases make our decisions for us, whether we want them to or not.

Some people don't believe that eternal staircases exist. They think staircases were just dreamt up by authority figures (parents, cops, local politicians) to scare kids out of loitering after dark. But that's what we're here for. To assure you that eternal staircases are very real—as is pretty much everything else you've been warned about.

∼

Four hundred thirty-eight. Four hundred thirty-nine. Four hundred forty. June stopped. She had never been any deeper than this, and she wasn't pushing it now. Something always stopped her here. She credited it to self-preservation instinct. Intellectually, she figured that whatever was farther down was just more of the same. More dark steps, jagged like a handsaw or a row of dog's teeth. But something in her body believed differently. A slight quickening of her pulse, a tightening in the stomach. Her muscles saying, *No.* Saying, *If you go farther, you might not come back.* Saying, *Here is an invisible line that must not be crossed.*

"You coming, baby girl?" Harebell trotted deeper into the well, just ahead of June. She looked back at June for only a second before continuing.

They'd been planning to do this forever—sneak in and spend a night inside the Staircase, no tourists, no creepy boss, only June and Harebell and the canyon of steps, the stars . . .

"This is a good spot." June plopped down on the four-hundred-fortieth stair. Her knees buzzed from the descent. The deeper they went, the more elastic the air became, the more her thoughts shuffled like playing cards. June pressed the heels of her palms into her eyes and tried to catch her breath. When she was a kid, ill with a fever, she called this sensation "Little/Big." Silence rattled too loud. Noise pinched to a muffle or clamped shut. Every object felt either impossibly minute or so leviathan it would devour her. Once, home sick from school, she became convinced that a loose thread on her pillow was multiplying so quickly it would bury the whole house.

"You all right, Junebug?"

"I'm fine." June shivered. "Let's sit down for a minute. C'mere."

Harebell slid down in front of June and leaned back so her head lolled in June's lap. In the shifting twilight, her hair seemed to be every color at once. They shared a pair of earbuds and looked at the stars. Joni Mitchell sang about clouds. Above them, real clouds undulated with moonlight, becoming wolves and sports cars. One looked like a bottle of hot sauce. One looked like June and Harebell, blended at the seams so they melted into each other like slivers of wet soap. One cloud looked like an exit sign, blinking. June fell asleep.

***

Warning: Some visitors to the Eternal Staircase experience a side effect called "step sickness," due to an optical illusion created by the attraction's unique geometry. Step-sick guests may be unable to tell if they are heading up the stairs or down the stairs.

Should you lose your directional orientation while visiting the Eternal Staircase, do not panic—

> there is a simple test you can do to find an exit. Simply remove one shoe and drop it on the nearest stair. Whichever way it falls is down. Walk in the opposite direction. Do not bother putting your shoe back on. Abandon it. There are other shoes in the world.
>
> (The Eternal Staircase management does not reimburse for lost shoes.)

When June awoke, she was hungry, and Harebell was gone.

"Hare?"

June's stomach growled. Or she thought it was her stomach. She couldn't be sure whether the hum rose from her body or from the belly of the Eternal Staircase. "Hare?" she called again. "Seriously, where are you?"

A figure emerged from below.

"Right here." Harebell was smiling, swaying from side to side. "Just exploring a little, don't freak out." It was too dark for June to see much more than an outline, but even in silhouette, something wasn't right. Harebell's limbs were too long, her fingertips almost dragging on the stairs. Her neck stretched double its length. June blinked. When she opened her eyes, the normal Harebell had returned.

Harebell had a plastic lighter in hand, which she flicked absentmindedly with a thumb. Light, dark. Light, dark. "God, I'm bored. Aren't you bored? All the hours we've spent scraping gum off these things"—she split into giggles—"working doubles. This cheap fucking place. And down there . . ." The lighter sparked. Light. Dark. Light. "Don't you want to know what's at the bottom?"

Harebell's eyes were glassy, her words slurred. Her hands trembled like leaves in summer rain. Each time she flicked the lighter on, the flame illuminated her for a moment, and with each illumination, June's heartbeat sped up. *Flash*—four protrusions jutted from Harebell's skull. *Horns* . . . The darkness returned. *Flash*—Harebell's eyes were gone—just smooth, pale skin where sockets should have been. *Flash*—Harebell was naked, and a grapefruit-sized hole had bloomed in her stomach—June could see right through it, to the staircase boring deeper and deeper beyond. *Flash. Flash. Flash.* Moving toward her, Harebell stumbled on a step and caught herself at June's feet. She dropped the lighter, and June grabbed it, stuffing it in her own pocket. In the steady darkness, Harebell's silhouette stopped its flickering. June's eyes adjusted again to the night. The horrors, gone. Just Harebell, shaking.

"Damn, Junie, you're so fucking beautiful. You know that? I love how beautiful you are."

"Come on." June hoisted Harebell up, an arm slung around her waist. "Let's get out of here."

Harebell gaped down into the Eternal Staircase. "But I haven't seen it down there," she muttered. "I haven't seen the bottom."

"Maybe some other time. But not tonight."

Harebell hissed at June like a street cat, and June reeled back. Harebell cracked into giggles again, a thin sound like a broken bicycle chain.

"Okay, Junie. If you want, baby, you can go back up."

"We're both going back up." June took Harebell's arm, and then, softer, she said, "Please, Hare. Please . . ." June kissed the shivering girl on the cheek. Harebell didn't argue after that.

June bore Harebell against her as they climbed back toward the rim. Going up was much harder than going down. June's heartbeat thudded against her ribs, Harebell's warm weight heavier than it should have been. A tug of war. June pulling one way, the Staircase dragging the other. Harebell looked behind her the whole way back.

✒

If pregnant, asthmatic, or prone to bouts of prolonged heartache, consult your doctor before visiting the Eternal Staircase.

Do not visit the Eternal Staircase with a sweetheart. They will grow to love the Eternal Staircase more than you. They will accidentally say the Eternal Staircase's name instead of yours while you're having sex.

Make the Eternal Staircase a part of your vacation today!

✒

Visitor, we'll tell you how it ends, though you already know. This story always ends the same way. Everyone hates the ending. But the story is told and retold anyhow.

One girl clocks in for work on a Tuesday night and never clocks out. She is officially marked as Disgraced in the employee register. For a few months, she's spotted now and then—trying to steal food from the hotdog stand, trailing her fingertips through dust gathered on sun-warmed steps, sleeping on the western rim. Splotches of hair dye stain the public restroom. But soon the sightings grow less frequent, then end altogether. The Eternal Staircase rumbles against midwinter winds, as if digesting a meal.

The other girl quits. Uses the money she's saved working at the Eternal Staircase to buy a cheap car with a wheezing radiator. Drives it away from the Staircase toward a far-off city. New York or LA. Gets a job writing for a lifestyle magazine, gets an apartment, a boyfriend. Dreams of Harebell still, some nights, but forgets upon waking.

At least, that's how we think the story ends. That's how it ended last time. Maybe this time it ends differently.

∽

If a stairwell leads down, it also leads up. It just depends on which direction you're walking.

∽

Come to the Eternal Staircase, insomniacs. Come, bored teenagers from the cages of your small towns. Come from your weeping. Come from your miles of driving through bleached desert, lush forest, from America's junkyards and factory lots. Come with your cursed maps. With your vices and wants. All highways lead to the Eternal Staircase if the Eternal Staircase wants you. Come, you who were born with the Eternal Staircase rocking you, a pull so strong it pulsed beside your own small heartbeat. Come into the blue-black light. Come closer. Walk with us.

We only offer this invitation out of politeness. In truth, the Eternal Staircase chooses who it swallows. And if called—you will come.

A DIVINER'S ABECEDARIAN

ALOMANCY
(divination by salt)

Before, salt was only for seasoning. It slept in porcelain shakers at our dinner tables, and we shook it over our plates without fear. We didn't heed the superstitions of spilt salt, or salt tossed over a shoulder. We paid no attention to the shapes in which the salt fell. We never collected salt in secret, didn't steal our mothers' novelty shakers shaped like tomatoes and houses and dogs, didn't hoard paper packets of salt from fast-food joints, or take it up in fistfuls to throw onto the flat earth. We didn't read the strange runes it formed against the soil. Things were different then. Objects only were what they were. Nothing more.

BIBLIOMANCY
(divination by book)

Imagine what our teachers would say if they knew what we'd done with our missing textbooks. Even worse, with the yearbook, each of our six photos tucked primly side by side, like scales on an ugly fish.

CYCLOMANCY
(divination by spinning objects)

We play spin the bottle with an empty two-liter soda jug. We don't mention how there aren't any boys here, in the carpeted basement of one of our mothers' houses. If we did, we'd shame ourselves out of playing. Our six sleeping bags are loose around us, shiny like sealskins. When we kiss one another, we do it quickly, as if touching our lips to an electric fence. Then we wipe our mouths on our hands and pretend so loudly that we hated it—that meeting softness in the circle of flashlight glow was only a chore, a duty we had to perform. We are servants to the rules we set.

One of us spins the plastic bottle and asks, *Which of us is the prettiest?* The bottle chooses the girl with the long blond hair we all envy, who pinks in the dim light. We imagine lighting her hair on fire. Her turn to spin. *Who's the ugliest?* and the one it points to shrinks as we titter into shivers. She tosses the bottle like a top. *Which of us is a liar?* she asks. It lands on the one in the ice-cream pajamas. Later that night, when the liar falls asleep, we write the word on her forehead with lipstick. Though she scrubs and scrubs all morning, the mark will not come off.

DRIRIMANCY
(divination by dripping blood)

The first one of us to bleed tells us not to set our morning alarms. *It will snow,* she tells us, *up to our hips. The school bus won't come.* We don't believe her, but when we look out our bedroom windows the world is smothered with snow, bright as a knife blade. We wade to her house and demand she show us how she knew. She says she won't, and we tear at our thighs, and we beg, and we lift our skirts and wait, but nothing happens.

FLEOMANCY
(divination by oil)

There is one of us whose mother packs her a lunch of olives with the pits still in them, housed in a little glass jar. She eats them with her fingers and wraps the pits in a soggy paper towel. It's disgusting. We call her Grease Girl. Her hands are always shiny, her notebooks smudged with oily fingerprints. She leaves handprints on her desk. We learned a long time ago not to look at the handprints. If we look, the handprints tell us things we don't want to know. Once, Grease Girl left a thumbprint on the dry-erase marker after writing an answer on the whiteboard in social studies class, and after Mr. Welkman saw it, he refused to speak for two whole weeks.

FLORIOGRAPHY
(divination by flowers)

Our school hosts a carnation sale every Valentine's Day. The student council sets up a folding plastic table in the science hallway and swaths it with a pink vinyl tablecloth and tops the pink vinyl tablecloth with house-painters' buckets frothing with flowers. The flowers cost one dollar a stem, or six for five dollars. There are pink carnations and white carnations and red carnations, and carnations fringed with blue and green and orange from having their stems placed in food coloring. All together, they look like a bowl of rainbow Cool Whip.

Each colored carnation means a different thing, so you can't buy just any. Pink means "friendship." White means "secret admirer." Red means "love." White with purple fringe means "I made a mistake." White with turquoise fringe means "There is someone in the parking lot." White with blue and yellow means "You will pack light and leave without telling anyone." Pink with orange fringe means "You will develop a lucrative kleptomania habit," while pink with scarlet fringe means "They know more than you think they do."

Ron Gorley buys a white carnation for the one of us with the big hoop earrings, which (1) is stupid because how can he be a "secret admirer" when he gave it to her in person and (2) is totally unfair because the one of us with the hoop earrings doesn't even like Ron Gorley, even though Ron Gorley is obviously the cutest guy in sixth grade, plus has a giant trampoline. Ron Gorley's white carnation is wasted on the one of us with the hoop earrings. We consider tugging on the hoops until her ears pop off.

GYROMANCY
(divination by dizziness)

Mr. Welkman tells us there's a new girl joining our class next week, so at recess, we hide behind the dodgeball wall and take turns pressing on one anothers' hearts until we pass out.

When we wake up, we are dizzy and not sure what time it is, and we have learned a lot about the New Girl. The New Girl will be moving here from Sacramento, and she will wear weird stretchy pants with paisley patterns on them, and we will hate her.

HIPPOMANCY
(divination by horse behavior)

Guess what? Horses don't actually have legs. Their legs . . . are really fingers. The one of us who takes riding lessons at Lilac Ridge Farm on Saturdays goes on to explain that a horse's thigh bone is actually hidden inside its torso. The part we think of as the shin is actually one gross long finger. The hoof is the nail. *You think they're these majestic, cute animals, but they aren't. They're creeps.*

One of us determines that this means horses are basically big, fast hands. We convince the one of us who is best at palm reading to sneak into the stable after school and see what she can find out. Later, after she breaks her leg crawling under a horse to look at its belly, her mom calls all our parents and we get grounded for a week. She's a snitch. We bet she isn't even as good at palm reading as she says she is. Snitches usually aren't good at much.

ICHNOMANCY
(divination by footprint)

The one of us with the broken leg has to drag herself around on crutches. The cast makes her footprints lopsided—one normal one and one fat round one like a Sasquatch track. We can only get half a read on her. For example, we know she is going to get sick at someone's birthday party, but we don't know whose. We refuse to invite her to any birthdays until the cast comes off. Her own birthday isn't necessarily ruled out, either, so when she passes out the pale yellow invitations, we throw every one of them away.

JYOTISHA
(divination by Hindu astrology)

On the day before the New Girl arrives, we sneak into the administration office after hours. We keep the lights off. The New Girl's admissions file is sealed up in a steel cabinet, but the one of us who inherited her granddad's pocketknife cracks open the lock. Now when the New Girl comes, we'll already know all we need to about her: *Born November 10. Vrschika, the scorpion. Ruled by Mars. Water sign. Fixed.*

And we'll know how to handle her.

KERAUNOMANCY
(divination by thunder and lightning)

A storm swells over the school, fat and pearly as a pool of concrete. We aren't allowed outside for recess because of the rain, so we're stuck in the English room watching *Schoolhouse Rock!* instead. Except we aren't watching *Schoolhouse Rock!* We're watching *her.* A tally:

- aforementioned tight paisley pants
- no bra, as far as we can tell (Doesn't she know we can see her nipples through that turtleneck?)
- purple ruler
- three pencils, sharpened, with the erasers chewed off
- an *NSYNC sticker on a blue-striped notebook
- Converse high-tops
- lime lip balm, reapplied every ten minutes

When lightning flashes across the paneled windows, we begin to count. None of us count out loud, but we can all hear the *tick, tick, tick* of the round clock screwed into the wall above the whiteboard. One second, two, three . . . We hold our breaths. We wait for thunder, bursting. *One for friend and two for rival, three for thief and four for an idol, five for never trust a word, six for following the herd, seven for a losing bet, eight for a storm you won't forget . . .* At the clock's ninth tick, a low rumble bellies over us. The windows wiggle against the sound waves.

LETNOMANCY
(divination by secrets)

We whisper things like: I heard the New Girl had to leave her old school 'cause she poked a kid's eye out with a stick. I heard the New Girl hasn't ever been to a movie theater. I heard the New Girl still sleeps in her mom's bed. I heard the New Girl showers only once a week and that's why her hair looks like that. I heard the New Girl doesn't show up to class on time or at all even, some days. I heard the New Girl doesn't show up in mirrors. I heard the New Girl has had a fever of 103.4 for two years, but they still let her come to school. I heard the New Girl is a loser. I heard the New Girl steals other kids' stuff and sells it. I heard the New Girl isn't even a girl, is something else, different from us, unnamable. I heard the New Girl eats peanuts with the shells still on them. I heard the New Girl is here, and isn't to be trusted.

MOROMANCY
(divination by foolishness)

We aren't stupid. We know she's just a kid. Like the six of us. But we also know she isn't like us, in all the ways that count. And we also know that being a sixth-grade girl doesn't mean you can't have a terrible sort of power. We know all about power. We've felt a heart stop under the pressure of our hands, and start up again. We've felt the weight of a horse's spooked body. We've learned things that none of our parents or teachers could ever learn. Things they wouldn't want to learn. We've spoken to the dead and watched hot wax congeal in pools of tap water.

We've burned locks of one another's hair and seen our own reflections in the smoke. We know how powerful a girl can be.

She plays dumb when we tug at her ugly clothes, when we whisper incantations behind her back, when we trip her in the halls. On the school bus, we dig little half-moons into her arms with our nails. And still, she acts like we're friends. We are not friends. We are not stupid. And neither is she.

NATIMANCY
(divination by buttocks)

Look, one of us has a better ass than the rest. It's just the truth. It's round and bouncy and jiggles like a cafeteria Jell-O cup. And okay, normally we'd say we hate the one of us with the good ass, because duh. But the truth is, the boys are always smacking it without her permission, which probably sucks. We find the one of us with the awesome ass crying in the farthest bathroom stall. She said Ron Gorley had slapped her butt when she was on her way to homeroom, so hard it left a welt. We hate Ron Gorley. Ron Gorley is the grossest, worst boy in school. We can't believe we ever thought he was cute.

The next day, the one of us with the great ass wears yoga pants to school. When we're in line to take our class picture, she stands right in front of Ron Gorley. Then she bends down to tie her shoe, really slowly so her ass is up in Ron Gorley's face like a big, beautiful planet for Ron Gorley to orbit. He lifts his hand, slingshots it back, and *smack*. When Ron Gorley makes contact, his eyes turn Elmer's-glue white. No pupils or iris at all, just blank and glossy. He coughs up white foam. He mumbles and mumbles and doesn't move. When he's taken to the school nurse on a gurney and his parents are called in, we can hear the nurse whispering to his father. *I don't know what's wrong,* she says. *He's hallucinating, but I don't know what he thinks he's seeing.*

We know exactly what he's seeing.

OMPHALOMANCY
(divination by navels)

For winter break, we all get our belly buttons pierced. At the piercing parlor in the mall, they make the hole with a hollow needle that scoops part of your belly flesh out with it before putting the metal ring through. At least, that's what the one of us with the sixteen-year-old sister tells us. Our parents make us invite the New Girl, but when it's her turn to get hers pierced, she chickens out. We're glad she does, because she's a loser and we don't want anything in common with her, and we don't want her to know what the hollow needle tells us.

The hollow needle tells us that pain is a tool. The hollow needle tells us that we are beautiful and eternal and that we will never die as long as we keep the wound clean and as long as we listen to the hollow needle. The hollow needle tells us that tomorrow, a bomb will fall on a city many thousands of miles away, and in another city, a kitten will be born with two heads. The hollow needle tells us to go ice-skating at the Retreat Meadows at 4 p.m. next Friday. It tells us to strap our skates tight, and it tells us to avoid the dark patch of the lake to the left of the ice-fishing huts. That our bellies are precious, jeweled creatures that will be harmed by the dark patch. The hollow needle whispers the sound of cracking ice to us, only to us, not to the New Girl.

PNEUMANCY
(divination by blowing)

We play Suck and Blow at the Chinese buffet with a plastic fortune-cookie wrapper. The goal is to pass the wrapper from mouth to mouth, only using the suction of our breath to keep it from fluttering to the floor. If it falls, you kiss by mistake. The one of us with the weird mole on her neck drops the wrapper next to Xavier Martins. We know she did it on purpose. Xavier Martins is the cutest boy in school (way cuter than Ron Gorley) and everyone knows it and the one of us with the weird mole on her neck is a cheater who doesn't deserve to kiss Xavier Martins.

The New Girl drops the wrapper, too. Of course. She's so terrible at *everything*. She kisses the one of us with the roller-skate shoes, and when she does, it's like she's kissing all of us at once (because ever since we got our belly buttons pierced, when something happens to one of us, it happens to all of us). And so at once, all of us see that the New Girl isn't going to be alive for much longer.

QABALAH
(divination by esoteric occultism)

The one of us with super-religious parents sneaks us into her father's library. We bring a bunch of kitchen herbs to burn in the trash bin. Then we hold hands and close our eyes, like witch girls do on TV. We ask if the New Girl is supposed to die. The smoke in the room says: *Yes.* We ask the smoke if we are supposed to help her die. The smoke says: *Yes.* We ask the smoke how. The smoke says: *Yes, Yes, Yes,* until the air is so thick that we cough and run out, leaving the flaming wastebasket behind.

RHABDOMANCY
(divination by sticks or wands)

To turn a baton just the right way, so it looks like it's twirling effortlessly flat like an airplane propeller, the wrist must move in small figure eights. Infinity symbols. *Infinity breeds infinity,* says the one of us who won first place in baton twirling at the Winter Carnival. We practice infinity for days. By the time we've perfected it, our batons move in perfect tandem, the tinsel on each end glinting like cut glass. We have mastered infinity. We can see what happens later, and what happened before we were born, because when we twirl our batons, all of time happens at once.

The New Girl can't hold the baton steady. She drops it at least nine times during our hour-long gym class. When she twirls it, it looks sloppy and doesn't move smoothly the way it should, not in a figure eight at all, so she is stuck right here in gym class and nowhere else in time. She can't see any further than today.

STYRAMANCY
(divination by chewing gum patterns)

The one of us with braces unwraps an entire package of Bubblicious strawberry bubble gum, all five pieces. We help her stuff them into her mouth. She chews until the five pieces are one fat, rosy glob. Pink as a tongue. How it threads through her braces like twine. How it spreads and nets and catches. She smiles, and a wire pops. She gapes her mouth wide as a coffin, wide as a lake. A red tangle. We read until our mouths go dry.

TRANSATAUMANCY
(divination by things accidentally seen or heard)

We have ears everywhere—by which we mean any object can listen if coaxed: a snapped hair tie abandoned in a bathroom; a CD jewel case; a Lisa Frank binder with a snow leopard on the front; a pair of earrings with surgical steel hooks. Anything we have touched can hear, can see, can tell us what it knows.

URANOMANCY
(divination by the sky)

We will call for the New Girl when the migrating songbirds are gone. When the dawn sun blushes like a peony over winter hills. There is a time for everything, and a sign for every time. A diviner knows this. Down here on the earth, it's hush-cold, sandpaper dragged over teeth.

Bike tires gone slack with the tightening air. Ground, half metal. But in the sky, it's colder.

The moon is swelling now, drawing in a great lustrous breath. This is what anticipation looks like. A black sky punctured by light, growing louder and louder. A mighty, dead rock, hovering over our girl-bodies. What if the moon were to fall? If it were to pass through us like a stone through a pane of glass? Through a gentle sheet of ice?

One of us claims that your period can sync up with the moon phases, but we think that's probably bullshit. If blood falls in step with anything, it's Mars. War planet. Red planet. Planet that looms and hollers and holds the tallest mountain in our solar system, which (according to Mr. Welkman) is a volcano called Olympus Mons that may or may not still be active.

VIDEOMANCY
(divination by films)

On the night before we kill the New Girl, the six of us go out to the movies. We buy small popcorns and boxes of Junior Mints. The movie has something to do with a bus driver who stumbles on a Masonic treasure, but we aren't watching for plot. We are watching for the sub-liminal stills that flicker between the frames. So quick, no one else sees. Halfway through, Xavier Martins leans over to kiss the one of us with the weird mole, and we all feel his lips graze her chin. We barely pause, the hidden movie stills flick, flick, flicking past.

WATER WITCHING
(divination by divining rod)

Two-pronged stick snapped from a dead tree by the Retreat Meadows. Hold it up, feel the tug. We leave boot marks in the blackened snow. We follow the *Y* toward water. Soon, she'll come.

XENOMANCY
(divination by strangers)

The New Girl might think she knows us—but she doesn't. If she did, she would have said no when we invited her to the Retreat Meadows at 4 p.m. on Friday. But she did not say no. Far from it. She thanked us.

When the New Girl arrives, she's all bundled up in snow pants and a puffy down jacket. The rest of us are in jeans. She even walks stupid, with her knees bowed out. She laughs at the wrong moments. She keeps talking about Sacramento, like any of us cares. Hanging out with her all day better be worth the trouble. It will be. It will be.

Out on the Meadows, the ice is murky. Fog gone solid. A dead fish lies frozen just below the surface. We levitate over it, we strange sharp creatures with blades on our feet, the alarms of our hearts bellowing, our exposed skin icy and pink. The New Girl wobbles. In the distance, fishing shacks creak into the wind.

A race! we call in one voice. We turn to the New Girl. *Last one to the blue shack is a loser!* We start to cut over the frozen water. The New Girl scrambles along. Catches stride. She becomes half bird, first a fledgling emerging from the nest, then an albatross, gliding. She picks up speed, passing us. She doesn't notice that the rest of us have stopped skating. Have fallen back to watch as she bullets toward the blue shack, toward the patch of dark ice. She's ten feet away, and a terrible grace has seized her. Five feet away, the horizon line zipped tight as a scar. Two feet, then one, and she reaches her mittened hand up toward the blue shack. A great crack rolls through the Meadows. The lake splits open. The New Girl is swallowed by the dark.

YDROMANCY
(divination by water gazing)

When the six of us pull the New Girl from the hole in the ice half an hour later, she is shiny and dead and ours. Her cheeks are blushed with frost and almost beautiful. Her lips are plump and pale. We take her home to our nearest mother's house. We dress her in our clothes. We comb her clean, wet hair. We pull a needle from our mother's sewing kit and we press it through the frostbitten skin of her navel, so cold not a drop of blood rises. We whisper into her mouth until she whispers back. We lead her to the mirror. When we are done, she looks just like us.

ZOOMANCY
(divination by animal behavior)

There are nights when wild animals still prowl outside our houses, but mostly they stay away. They know the true alphas of this town. The seven of us howl along to the radio. We paint our nails a matching plum red. We take what prey comes to us: boys who ask too many questions; teachers who try to tell us what to do. Nothing is a surprise to us. We can read any omen—an orange sky, a rotten peach, a stained T-shirt, a pop song on loop, a kiss-and-tell, a dropped phone call. When new girls come, we know what to do with them. We know how to fix them. We have a way of knowing every good thing there is to know.

The Thread Boy

THE WITCH WANTED A child, so he went to market and bought a spool of every color thread he could find. He bought silk thread and cotton thread and waxed linen thread and thread spun from wool. Scarlets and golds and bone whites and blues and burgundies. When he returned home, the witch poured his shopping sack out on the floor and unraveled the spools one by one. Then he matted the mass of thread together into the shape of a boy.

The Thread Boy was a hard worker and a loyal son. He tended the goats and chickens and helped nail boards over leaks in the roof. When his father was away at market selling turnips and potions, the Thread Boy would prepare thick venison stews, the scent of spices stitching through the whole house. At night, when the witch came home, he would tell his son wondrous stories over supper—stories about whaling ships off the eastern coast or cities with buildings so tall they punctured the sky. He told the Thread Boy about the railroads and highways that turned the country into a warped loom of motion. The more the Thread Boy listened, the more he knew he had to see it all for himself.

On the Thread Boy's seventeenth birthday, the witch conjured a pickup truck from a stack of hay bales. He gave the Thread Boy a sturdy backpack, the newest edition of every map the witch could find, and a tin full of postage stamps, so his son might write home to tell of his adventures. When the Thread Boy hugged his father goodbye, a single green thread caught on one of the witch's coat buttons. As the Thread Boy got into his new truck and drove away, the thread stretched outward, longer and longer, between the witch's button and wherever the Thread Boy was—and the witch was glad, for he knew that now his son would always be able to find his way home.

Each day, the Thread Boy drove until dusk, and at night he slept in the pickup bed. He saw wheat towns and corn towns, ghost towns and factory towns with top hats of black smog. The highway stretched ever onward. He drove through all his father's stories, and then into stories even his father didn't know. He might have continued this way forever, but his truck broke down in a coastal fishing village fifteen hundred miles from home; not even magic trucks are safe from a blown clutch.

The Thread Boy got a job as a dishwasher in a restaurant that sold the local catch. Each morning, fishermen would plop a sack of fresh fish onto the chef's counter while the Thread Boy scrubbed pots in the corner. Every day of the workweek brought a different fisherman.

Mondays: the quiet fisherman with the purple hat. Tuesdays: the crab fishermen, whose hands were scarred with claw marks. Wednesdays: the brothers with matching red beards. Thursdays: the salmon seller with a lisp. But it was Friday that was the Thread Boy's favorite day, for that was when the deep-sea captain came with her tub of monsters. Those fish had long teeth and jellied skin through which you could see their insides. Some had little lights flickering on the ends of antennae. Others had mouths so wide they looked like they were singing an aria. The chef always scrunched up his nose and grimaced at the sight of them. *Come on, Lucy, we can't sell this stuff! These fish are too ugly to cook. No one'll eat 'em. Don't you got anything else?* But the Thread Boy didn't think the fish were ugly. He thought they were beautiful. And he thought the captain was beautiful, too.

∽

The Thread Boy and Captain Lucy were lying on her boat. The Thread Boy was kissing Lucy's arms and hands and throat and the boat was rocking a little on the high tide. Lucy kept getting frays of cotton stuck on her tongue when she kissed him, which embarrassed the Thread Boy, but Lucy didn't seem to mind. She coaxed the Thread Boy to slip his hand up under her skirt, and the Thread Boy was amazed to find something even softer than he was.

The next morning, Lucy left for a fishing expedition. Before she went, the Thread Boy gifted her the end of one of his threads to wear around her wrist. It was a thin red thread, which stretched out from the Thread Boy's chest across the sea as Lucy's boat sailed away. All week, he could feel the small tug of it. On stormy days, it yanked wildly, and he knew Lucy's boat was on choppy waters. On placid days, it swayed softly in the air like a telephone line. Some nights, the thread grew so taut and firm that the Thread Boy could pluck it like a harp string.

When Lucy returned, the Thread Boy was relieved at the slackening. They once again spent long nights on her boat's deck, where Lucy would show him all the fantastical, terrible creatures she had stolen from the sea. On Fridays, Lucy would linger until the Thread Boy had finished the dishes, and they would make out in the walk-in freezer, surrounded by stacks of dead trout and plump cabbage heads.

Yet Lucy always had to leave again. There were always more monsters to catch, and her dedicated crew to lead. First, it was only for a few days or a week. Then the voyages grew longer and longer, her ship reaching farther across the waters. The trips stretched into many weeks, then months. Eventually, she stopped coming back at all. Not even on Fridays. The Thread Boy could still feel her move, the red thread dragging on him in a constant ache. But what could he do?

～

By then, he'd saved up enough to fix his truck. He quit his job at the restaurant, not even noticing when a thread snagged on the doorknob as he left. He drove west. In the rearview mirror, the interstate unraveled in silver ribbons. He picked up two hitchhikers at a tollbooth with whom he traveled for a few weeks. One carried a banjo, the other, an accordion, and their clothes were covered in patches embroidered with images of antlers and moths and train cars. The Thread Boy had never seen thread used this way before, and he marveled at the strange beauty his own matter could produce. The hitchhikers taught him their favorite songs, and how to tell fortunes by tossing rabbits' bones, and the Thread Boy taught them about the most frightening species of deep-sea fish. When at last he dropped them at their friend's apartment in the city, they each left with a new gray thread tied to their backpacks.

The Thread Boy snagged on more and more as time went on. One thread caught on a thunderous view overlooking a canyon. Another, on the World's Largest Ball of Twine: a roadside attraction, which, had he the words for it, he might have called God. Another three threads caught on the trio of mutts he helped a mechanic raise the next time his truck broke down. There were more beautiful girls, too, who always seemed stickier than other people, easier to snare, as if made of Velcro—the pale-haired dancer whose feet twitched as she slept; the radish farmer who could say *thread* in seven languages; the anthropology student with exactly seventy-five brown freckles on each cheek. More and more and more small hooks on which his thread caught and stretched outward from his body. More harp strings that yanked him here or there, which grew tighter the farther he moved from whatever or whomever he was tied to.

The Thread Boy became a tapestry. He grew so lost in the pull of his own skin that he could barely see outside the snarl of it. He moved slowly now, for when he walked in one direction, there was always a thread pulling the other way. Step forward to let one thread slacken, and another tightened. People had to climb over knots to get to him. He had trouble getting in and out of his truck, and before long, the thread started catching in the tires and windshield wipers, rendering him unable to drive any longer. Thus, the Thread Boy stopped his journeying, and lay again in the pickup bed, suspended by the hammock of his own body.

～

The witch missed his son. They had been parted for many years, and the Thread Boy had not written nearly as many letters as the witch would have liked. The witch took hold of the green thread wrapped around his button and he followed it over mountains and creeks, across busy overpasses and in and out of hamlets. He wound the thread into a neat ball as he went. When he finally reached his son, he could barely find him among the spears of red and gold and bone-white string. *Son,* said the witch, *when you were young you moved swiftly and untethered. It pains me to see you so bound. If you want, I can free you from this.* And the witch pulled a pair of silver shears from his sack, which he gave to the Thread Boy.

The shears were so well polished that the Thread Boy could see his reflection in the closed blades. They were cold and clean to the touch, and the Thread Boy squirmed against his ties. He could be free again. Just an unhitched hunger bulleting across the land. He would feel no more ache. No more drag on his low rib when the captain's boat docked in a new port, or the fish shop door slammed shut, or the hitchhikers hopped a southbound train. Leash-less.

Somewhere a mile off, a crow landed on a length of thread, and a single sweet note rose from the plucking. It traveled up the thread until it reached the Thread Boy, and as if summoned by the sound, a nearby cloud split open into a tumult of hail. Hailstones fell, fat as grapes. They bounced off the tightened threads, *plink, plink,* until the Thread Boy was wrapped in the most beautiful music, and he wept, and dropped the shears, unused. And he would not lift them again—not for anything.

Fox Jaw

YOU COME TO ME as a fox.

I'm on the stoop below my apartment writing a story about Mars, and when I look up, there you are. "The cocktail party last night was lovely," I say. "We drank mint juleps and talked about bad cinema and I told my friends you weren't coming, even though none of them asked." You are a fat little fox; you must be well-fed. You must visit many women who feed you full loaves of bread and kill chickens for you and sometimes let you eat them whole, too. You are a tiny Mars, all orange and plump with all those women. I toss you my pencil to chew on, but you don't seem to want it.

That night, when you come to me as yourself, you don't mention being a fox earlier, so neither do I. If I did, I would have to say something about how many women it looked like you ate, and we agreed that the fastest way to kill the mood is to talk about the other women. Instead, we watch TV. When we fuck, I pretend I am a fox. I imagine triangular ears and soft black mittens and pointy teeth. I bite your shoulder to test them. Foxes don't fall in love with anyone. Foxes don't even have a word for love. If you were to ask a fox if he loved you, he would probably eat you, but not for the reasons you might hope.

○

I decide to make Mars like the Czech Republic. *National Geographic Magazine* once printed a photo of a church in the Czech Republic built from human bones, with skulls stacked one on top of the other against the walls and a chandelier made of femurs. This is exactly the kind of place I want there to be on my Mars, so I write it into the story. Instead of a church, it's the supermarket that's made of bones, with skulls piled where the cantaloupes would normally be. Martians don't shop there, though, like in an Earth supermarket. They go there to drop off the skeletons of old sweethearts. There's a machine they feed the bones into piece by piece, like those machines they have in Earth supermarkets for recycling bottles. When a Martian finishes dropping their lover into the machine, a small blue token pops out. They keep the token in their wallet or in the basket with their car keys until they find a new sweetheart, and then the token just seems to get lost somewhere.

○

When your father comes to my work, I serve him dark roast coffee and a lemon bar on real porcelain dishes. Usually I give the customers paper cups so I don't have to wash so many mugs, but he helped make you, so I give him the real thing.

"I hear you're moving," your father says.

"Yes," I say, "I'm leaving in six weeks."

"I can see why he wouldn't want to get too invested in you," he says.

I don't say anything. I don't tell him that sometimes his son is not a man but a fox. I don't tell him about the time his son and I walked along the railroad in the snow, and an opossum crossed in front of us, and then we went home and made love on my living room floor.

"Where are you moving to?" he asks.

"Mars," I say.

He laughs like I'm joking.

When I refill his coffee, I give it to him in a paper cup.

〜

After work, I go to my favorite tea shop to write about Mars some more. The shop is underground, in the basement of a place that gives massages. I wonder if the massage parlor upstairs gives happy endings. I wonder if they could give us one, in the literal sense, if I ask them nicely and offer to help edit all the masseuses' manuscripts.

I order strawberry crème tea and settle in an armchair in the corner. I think I'm going to make my Martian protagonist a banker. She will spend all day behind a counter in an air-conditioned room and will be too busy counting to have any sweethearts. She won't even know about the supermarket full of bones because she'll never have a reason to go there. She will wear her hair in a tight braid atop her head and she'll have a small plaque at her desk with her name etched into it. Polly, maybe. Or Joanne. Or maybe her name is my name. Maybe it's yours.

She has a photo calendar on her desk with a different animal for every month. They are all Martian animals, so some of them have six legs, or two heads, or are just orbs of energy that float in empty swimming pools. One day, she'll look at her calendar and realize all the Martian animals in the photos have been replaced with foxes. She'll have never seen a fox before, because they don't have foxes on Mars. Maybe she'll scream. Maybe she'll take off all her clothes and lie down on the teller counter, even though the bank is still open and a customer is waiting. Maybe she'll ignore the foxes and just keep counting money.

My only set of married friends goes out for dinner, and asks me to watch their six-year-old son, Jesse. He and I bash bricks onto the concrete driveway. Jesse says the red dust that chips from the bricks is fairy dust. He says that if you plant birdseed in the garden, a baby bird will grow. I think Jesse knows more about how things really work than most people do. Definitely more than me. Jesse asks if my painted fingernails are real. He says he likes fake nails better than real ones, because you can spread fake nails around a room, and you can drop fake nails in a swimming pool so they drown. Then you have to put on goggles to swim down and find them all, which he says is one of the hardest games in the world.

That night, I dream that I am pulling off my fingernails and giving them to you. You toss them into a lake, and as they sink to the bottom you make a wish on each one. For a moment, I am angry; shouldn't I get to wish on my own nails? But then you turn and I see your face and forget about being angry. I give you the last of my fingernails.

When the final one reaches the lake bottom, you do not put on goggles and try to retrieve them. Instead, you reach out your hand to me, asking for more. I only had ten, and you threw them all in the lake, so I start giving you other parts of my body—my hands and feet, my teeth, the caps on my knees. Eventually, you get bored and go inside without diving in for any of them. I would do it myself, but you already threw in my arms, so I wouldn't be able to pick any parts of me up or swim back to the surface. I just wait on the shore looking into the water until I wake up.

∽

Okay, so I wasn't supposed to love you. But I do, and this is why:

Because of that one time we lay on my futon mattress and listened to a radio play about a man who sold his soul to the devil.

Because you write poems about me and hide them in the freezer.

Because after I knocked a glass bottle out the fourth-story window and it shattered in the street, you made me go downstairs and sweep it up. Without you, I would have left it there.

∽

It's true—you can't really be angry with someone without loving them first. Sort of the way that you can't cook a meal without heating the pan. You have to care to the point that the grease starts spitting up at you in pin-pricks, and then, only then, can the anger start.

It is the fourth time you have stood me up this week. Dinner is cold on the table. I am done forgiving you and done listening to apologies, so I say nothing as you reheat our food in a cast-iron skillet. Lately, I have found myself wanting to make a fox-skin coat. I want to grab fox-you by the tail and slit right up the belly with a paring knife like you were an avocado or some kind of fruit, and then I would yank your skin right off. I would probably salt it and hang it in my window for a few weeks, so it would dry without rotting and so all the neighbors would see how clean a job I did. Then I would stitch you up with tight little stitches that wouldn't come loose, and sew white bone buttons down the middle. I would wear the coat when I ran errands—to buy more toothpaste and shampoo, since you used all mine, or to go to the dentist. If I wore it to a job interview, the employer would be so impressed with my take-charge attitude that I'd get the job. Your boss would see me downtown, and he'd give me your job, too, and ask me out for drinks. I would collect so many jobs and admirers I would have to install wide pockets into the coat, just to stow them all comfortably.

Sometimes, though, I feel like you got there first—that I am a jacket slung over your shoulder. Sometimes I feel like I am a jacket you draped over a beehive, with bees swarming in my sinuses and under my tongue and sticking to my stomach lining. Sometimes I find photos of you in my pockets, and don't remember placing them there. Sometimes I reach into a pocket to look for my keys, and find a fox bite, instead.

∼

I get home late from work. You are already asleep, your lean body roped across our mattress, the bedsheet thrown off save for a twist of linen around your left calf. When I slip into bed beside you, light from a streetlamp licks your cheek through the window. You begin to flicker. Scarlet fur sprouts from your shoulders and then vanishes. Your hands flash between fingers and paws. The fabric around your ankle becomes a tail, then a bedsheet again, then a tail, the tip like a wet paintbrush, then back to linen. This is how you look unguarded. Bristling between your many selves as you breathe in and out, unaware that I, beside you, am watching.

I can't sleep. Instead, I pack my life into crates. First, my dresses, which I roll up into little dumplings and stuff into a suitcase. Then my books, which I stack into cardboard boxes only after reading the last page of each. I keep hoping for optimistic endings, but most of them end with someone drowning or leaving home or with the family farm being bought out by a luxury sports car salesman. My sewing supplies are the next to go—twill, poplin, corduroy, silk, gabardine, and under the last bolt of lace, a shirt of yours with a hole in the shoulder. You had asked me to fix it months ago. Instead, I hide it in the bottom of the box. Across the room, you are still transforming in the lamplight. Each time your skin shocks with fur, you murmur. Does it hurt when you change like that? When your teeth sharpen, do they cut your tongue?

∿

Three days later, I leave. Instead of saying "goodbye," I say all my favorite words: "honeycomb, penumbra, avarice, bottle cap." You repeat them back to me. We stand there in the doorway of my empty apartment, speaking the same words back and forth until my throat gives up, and there is nothing left to do but go.

∿

Alone in the airport, I leave the Martians to themselves and instead write a story about a fox who never learned to shapeshift. All foxes can shapeshift, of course, even normal foxes, even foxes that no one is in love with. In this particular story, though, the truth is bent a little, and the protagonist is a fox that cannot shapeshift, and has to be in fox form all the time. This fox tries to follow along with the other foxes, but when it starts to rain, he can't turn into an umbrella, and when it gets too hot, he can't turn into a ceiling fan. In the end, the foxes all go on a hen hunt, and when the farmer shows up, all the other foxes turn themselves into kitchen appliances. The main fox stays a fox, though, so the farmer catches him and kills him and uses the fox–kitchen appliances to cook him up for dinner.

The story has no purpose. At least, not one I can identify. This is certainly for the best. Purposeless stories don't remind me of you, and, more importantly, don't remind me of myself. They just leave me alone with words slapped end to end in constant vibration, like those perpetual-motion toys made of stainless-steel balls on strings. Back and forth and back and forth, without destination.

∽

There are three vending machines in airport terminal 1K. The first two hold snack foods. The third is full of soda in plastic bottles. The bottles are lined up in the machine like a miniature army in matching red uniforms, and a sign on the front of the machine says THIRSTY? in blocky white letters. How clever. Even if you weren't thirsty before, you'll read that question and ask yourself, "Oh, am I thirsty?" and of course the answer will be yes, because we are always thirsty for something. Then you'll go buy a soda, even if the thing you are thirsty for isn't a soda at all. Soda might be second best.

A woman approaches the first snack machine and feeds a few coins into the change slot. It makes a whirring sound as if readying to launch off the ground. I imagine an airport vending machine must get jealous seeing airplanes fly all over the world, while they have to stay here and serve people bacon-flavored pretzels.

The woman presses three buttons and waits for her bounty. Something invisible lands behind the small door. For a moment, it could be anything. Perhaps it's a lucky rabbit's paw, or a tangerine, or a planet. It could be a bundle of letters, all stamped and addressed and ready to deliver. I wonder if one of the letters might be for me and, if so, would the woman let me read it even though she technically paid for it.

She kneels down to open the door—and for one excruciating moment, I am so sure that she'll reach in for her snack and, instead, pull out you. Your hair will be a bit mussed up and you'll be shivering, because it's refrigerated in there and you've been waiting a while. Then you'll run straight over to the bench I'd been watching from and we'd make out in front of everyone, and keep right on making out even when security asks us to stop.

The woman pulls her hand out from the vending machine. She is holding a granola bar. Cherry and yogurt.

∽

It has now been a month since I saw you. In that time, I've decided that the Martians have invented a teleportation device. Due to this new separation of time and space, the Martian populace had to find an efficient way to dispose of all the old vehicles. A few they kept, like Zambonis and lawn mowers—anything that had a purpose other than moving from point A to point B. But the rest had to go. Cars, trucks, buses, trams, trains, airplanes, ski lifts, golf carts . . . One politician suggested collecting them all together into an automotive history museum, but the Martians found this far too sentimental. Martians are not a nostalgic people. Enamored with their new technology, they felt it would be crass to reminisce about the time before: the Age of Yearning.

In the end, they collected all the vehicles and melted them down. The metal was used to make cutlery and belt buckles. Some of the tires became pencil erasers.

These days, the Martian language has no word for "distance," as distance has become obsolete. The Martian dictionary has removed many words since the invention of teleportation: *far, road, travel, away, homesick, lost.* The word for "ocean" is the same as the word for "footstep." The word for "gone" is also the word for "dead" and the word for "loveless." Martian children no longer dream of running away from home, of joining a band of mimes and living in the forest. Instead, they dream of the next life.

⌘

I decide to send you a package, so I go out to search for an appropriate gift. In a nearby craft market there is an artist selling sculptures made from cardboard. There is a cardboard hot-air balloon and a cardboard city and a man made of cardboard holding a cardboard telephone. In the back of the booth, beneath a cardboard speech bubble that says, "I really wish you wouldn't," I find a small cardboard fox. His head is about the size of my fists put together, and he rests on one bushy arm, which is thick with curls of finely snipped cardboard fur. His ears jaunt upward as if they are not fox ears at all, but rather two people embarking on a promising first date. The fox's eyes are half-lidded. Perhaps if he ever fully falls asleep, his ears will kiss over the dinner table of his head and start making each other promises neither of them intend to keep.

The artist makes me a cardboard box out of scraps from other cardboard boxes, specifically to fit the fox sculpture. I tell her I have to ship it overseas. "It shouldn't be a problem," she says. "That one's particularly robust."

Later that night, I find a fox mandible at the foot of an old tree. The teeth still peak in fine points. The bone curves like a spoon and is as pale as the white underside of my wrist. It looks just like you, but then again, everything I see looks like you. The strangest things have changed since I left. I see a fox in a shop or on the back of a book or decayed on the forest floor, and I write you one thousand letters. I lift a fox jaw from the earth and I want to climb inside like it's a small boat. Like it could carry me to you.

My Martian banker has a house made of Plexiglas. This is not abnormal in Martian society—Martians don't have the same squeamishness about privacy that we do. She eats breakfast in her kitchen while watching all her neighbors eat similar breakfasts in similar kitchens, straight through their clear Plexiglas walls. She presses her work clothes and licks envelopes and brushes her teeth, all the while watching her neighbors while her neighbors watch her.

The Martian banker never wonders what anyone is thinking, because all the Martians are made of Plexiglas, too. Underneath their skin, adrenaline and endorphins and other emotion-causing chemicals flow in bright colors. Electrical pulses flood the body in small runway lights. Anyone with basic chemistry knowledge and a good eye can look at a fellow Martian and know exactly what they're feeling. All the bankers are also chemists. There are no bank robberies, because adrenaline would throb neon through a robber's jugular and give them away. It is rare to be lied to. Lies are too colorful. The vibrancy is difficult to miss.

Though my banker has no time for lovers, she knows what love looks like. It is acid green. When it presses through the veins, it gives off static storms with sharp little lights. The banker has always thought that sweethearts looked like cactuses. She could never imagine what draws them to each other—the more in love they grow, the more cactus-like they become. With each pulse of love, they appear more and more painful to the touch.

~

I visit the bone church I had seen in *National Geographic*. It's in a small village an hour outside Prague, and is just as full of dead people as I imagined it would be. There are forty thousand skeletons. They have all been taken apart and rearranged into candleholders and garlands and a massive coat of arms, with a crow made of human bones pecking at a human made of human bones on the bottom right of the crest. The church is full of tourists taking photographs, and some Australians are listening to a guided tour. When no one is looking, I touch one of the skulls. I run my hand over the top of it, petting it like a small, cold cat. If I could go back in time and tell whoever's skull I am petting that one day, their bones would be arranged into church decor and a twenty-first-century person would be petting their skull like a cat, they probably wouldn't believe me. I like to think they wouldn't even listen to me in the first place. Hopefully they would have been too busy eating vegetable stew or having sex or walking along a river—all those things you can do when you're alive and a human and not a church decoration.

As I stop petting the skull, I notice that a few teeth are left in its jaw. No one saw me touch the skull. No one is watching me at all. I tug a tooth loose and slip it in my pocket. It settles next to the fox mandible I found in the woods. I realize that if I lived on Mars, I would never visit the supermarket. I have never returned a recyclable lover in my life. I just collect them in my pockets and let my pockets get heavier and heavier every year. Once in a while, I pull all my old lovers out and line them up in neat rows.

The tooth in my pocket was probably late for dinner one night. Its sweetheart would have waited until the candles burned down, bread going stale on the countertop. When the tooth arrived home, its sweetheart wouldn't speak to it for two hours, until the tooth kissed the words from its sweetheart's throat. Though the sweetheart was still angry, the tooth kept kissing it and saying "I'm sorry, I'm sorry," until they both started laughing and the stale bread didn't really matter to either of them.

But they are both dead now. The tooth is in my jacket pocket, and who knows where the sweetheart is. Probably nowhere, anymore. As I leave the church, the tooth clicks against the fox jaw in soft little taps—*tick, tick, tick,* like a clock.

The War of Fog

‖: THE WAR OF FOG *lasted for nine days, falling between the Cartographers' War and the War of Small Regrets. Though ultimately the War of Fog would beget fewer widows than either the former or the latter, the War of Fog left a deeper haunting on the people. Historians have archived sixfold as many nightmares about the War of Fog than Cartographers' or Small Regrets combined. Even the War of Nightmares logged, ironically, fewer nightmares than the War of Fog. Thus, some refer colloquially to the veterans of the War of Fog as "Alley Cats" for their nocturnal, insomniac ways—and for the feral yowling those who remember make in the night.*

∽

Those are my father's words. He raised me alone, in the largest city in Beldule. "City," I admit, is informed more by our own pride than a worthy population. Camello cradles no more than seven thousand residents—a village, really—ribboned with dirt roads that tie in neat bows around peacock-colored hills, dotted with long-haired goats. My father is an academic, though Camello has never had a university. Or rather, it once had a university of two: my father, and his incompetent, dark-haired typist, Oreno. My father dictated his philosophies while Oreno pounded two-fingered onto an electric typewriter. I paid little attention to my father's theories then. Why listen to an old man ramble on about old battles, when I could be feeding crabapples to the neighbor's guinea hens and mudlarking for blue glass in the creek? But then Oreno left for the war (imagine, that piglet Oreno as a soldier—ha!), and the role of stenographer fell to me.

I hate the whirr and clack of the typewriter keys, like enlivened dentists' tools plucked from a sterile tray. My father's treatises on the Second Eternity bore me to stone, and he often resorts to smacking me awake with his baton (a long birch switch with which he draws invisible charts in the air to consolidate his thoughts).

I love my father, but I do not enjoy him. This combination occurs not infrequently. The more I grow to love a man, the less I tend to like him.

The Army of Fog, by the numbers, was formidable: eighty times greater than any Jasmine Age army, and leagues more technologically advanced. The Army of Fog's cannonballs, for reference, were two thousand pounds each—while the Neolideans' (during the War of False Drums) weighed only twelve. Imagine. Imagine! You cannot. War cannot be imagined, for those who have not witnessed it cannot truly fathom it, and for those who have borne witness—it is no longer an imagining. It is a boot print permanently crushed into the heart.

There was, despite the name, no fog in the War of Fog. The August in question was unseasonably clear. No dew pocked the late lilies, nor did a single cloud obscure the sky above Camello. The war's title refers, instead, to a singular optical illusion. The Army of Fog, in addition to its unprecedented size, was meticulously trained—so when the uniformed troops, garbed in gray gabardine, marched in unbroken rows through the agricultural countryside of Beldule, they appeared at a distance not as a collection of men, but as a single silver bank of fog, pouring over the land. The army was so large, that to a civilian watching the approach from a café window, the procession continued uninterrupted for all nine days of the war.

(Author's note: To interject a personal voice into this account—I myself witnessed the invasion in just such a manner through a café window. As the soldiers passed, I drank one cup of coffee. Then two. The soldiers seemed as one snaking shadow. An hour passed, and another hour, and another. Still, their ranks flowed unfractured. Four. Five. The coffee ran low. Nine hours. We slept on the floor. I ate a small cake topped with raspberries, and then vomited into the sink. The Army of Fog blurred and ebbed. A day went by. We began to believe it would never end. The Army of Fog, an eternity, or perhaps even an Eternity. The few of us clustered in the café grew increasingly liberal with our speculations. Perhaps the soldiers were not men at all, but rather boiled up from some lake in the north and would continue flowing until the lake bed ran dry. One woman, desperate to keep her toddler at ease, insisted to him that the mass was a great, enveloping—

Sometimes, my father's dictations end in the middle of a sentence. He'll fall silent, a thought incomplete, and stare at the wall as if he were somewhere else. I don't mind this. The sooner his thoughts stall each day, the sooner I can continue combing the creek for blue glass.

When my mother (who I never knew) died, she left my father a small music box—and last week, on my fourteenth birthday, he passed it to me. Lifting the lid reveals a tiny painter in a tiny smock, who rises and spins. If you wind a key in a slot in the box's left side, the painter sweeps his miniature paintbrush up and down, up and down. Put a fingertip to the brush, and it leaves a small streak of real paint behind.

When I was young, I believed this was magic. Now that I am older, I know it must be a science I do not yet understand—which is only another way to say "magic."

It is into this box that I place my pieces of blue glass. My most treasured piece is a perfect crescent the size of my thumb. It fits perfectly beside the little painter, glinting like a fish. My goal for this summer: find one piece of glass per day, so that my collection will come to form a kind of chronicle. Each fragment, a fragment of me. Isn't it true that every sliver of glass in the box has been selected by a past version of myself? A self who spotted a flash of color and reached for it? A me that made a choice?

The glass winks up at me like a broken sky, the little painter working his sorcery in its midst.

∽

Let it not be said that the Beldulians accepted the Army of Fog's advance like heeling dogs. A mere hour into the first day, Beldule collapsed fifty-four of its own bridges, rendering the waterways impassable by foot or by boat. The Army of Fog was slowed, if not deterred. Unfortunately, this also made it impossible for civilians to flee. They huddled instead in their homes, watching the Army of Fog pass.

And pass. And pass. And pass. And pass. And pass. And pass.

∽

"It's simply gears. Like a clock, see?" Oreno tries to take the box from me. I snap the lid shut on his fat pinkie.

"Careful—if I lose my fingers, you'll have to do your father's typing instead, and I'll get to lie around eating bonbons, convalescing." He winks at me, one charcoal eye vanishing beneath long lashes.

I open the box, letting him free. The painter turns.

"Don't you have work to do? Surely my father is waiting."

Oreno's face goes dumb as a trout then. His eyes glaze in the same way my father's do when he fails to finish a thought.

"I am gone," Oreno whispers. He holds a hand to his stomach. His lips, soft and pale as if they had never been touched.

My father believes he himself is the chronicler in our family, but he is wrong. I am the one taking note of the things that matter.

∽

(Author's note: On the third day, the café proprietor—a stout man with a broom-like mustache—closed all the blinds. No one spoke it aloud, but we were grateful. By then, watching the

advance had given way to an excruciating boredom. Humans can grow bored of all things, somehow. This is one of our great blessings. They say that art, that beauty, is what allows us to endure times of great horror—but no. It is our bottomless capacity for boredom.

Eventually, I would return home, to attend to my daughter and to my work. Or so I would tell myself. In honesty, it was the boredom that drove me at last from the café. A shaking, unquenchable boredom.

I'll admit for the first few hours of the war, I was entranced. The way the Army of Fog undulated—it was like a team of synchronized swimmers, so precise in their motion, but also like water itself. Yes, in the beginning, I found the Army of Fog to be almost beautiful.

My god. Forgive me.)

The little painter is playing tricks on me.

When I open my box, fistfuls of blue glass are missing.

I push into my father's study without knocking, a forbidden action that will earn me at worst a lashing and at best a practiced scowl. Oreno is behind his typewriter as usual.

"You stole from my music box," I accuse.

His hands stall on the keys like a pair of frightened deer.

"Give it back." I try to crease my brow like my father does when he's angry.

"I did no such thing," Oreno says—more to my father than to me. "First, I have no interest in children's trinkets. Second, how could I possibly take your belongings when I am away in the war? In fact, at this very moment,

I am entering the battle on Greenmount, from which I won't return."

My father shoos me from the room. He locks the door behind. Oreno's clumsy typing follows me all the way back to my chamber, pattering like gunfire.

I know my collection intimately. The crescent. The piece shaped like a mushroom. The piece shaped like a bat. The piece shaped like Oreno's chipped front tooth. The piece shaped like a horseshoe. Strangely, when I take stock of what remains, the only shards removed are the ones added over the last nine days—as if they had never been added at all.

⌇

One of the greatest tragedies of the War of Fog is that it seems to have been fought for no true purpose. Unlike the holy Wars of Quartz, or the moral obligation necessitated by the Orphan War and the War of Scarlet Rope, the War of Fog was driven neither by faith nor by humanitarianism. It lacked even the base motive of border expansion, colonialism, or other such matters of state.

The War of Fog was triggered by a single errant assassination. Due to a complex system of allegiances (established between nations decades earlier, as part of the peace accords following the War of Plenty), this assassination set off a chain reaction, and the levers and pulleys holding the world's sovereign nations together snapped. The accords collapsed into little more than string-snipped marionettes, slumped and lifeless. The War of Fog began.

The title, then, of the War of Fog, proved to be appropriate in more ways than one. It is a war with no body. No motive. Only mist.

(Author's note: At the time, we did not call it the War of Fog. Historians assigned that moniker later, with distance and forget-

ting. Those of us who lived it called it by the same name the Cartographers' War and the War of Small Regrets and the Orphan
War and the War of Scarlet Rope and all the others were con-
temporaneously called. Those who live through such times call
them not by their proper titles. We refer to them only as "the
War." This is because one experiencing war cannot fathom that
anyone else in history has ever existed in such a heightened state
as this. Though we know, through logic and reason and literary
documentation, that we are not, in fact, singular—the heart disagrees. No war could be more sanguinary. More storied. Yes, this
is The War. The only war that ever has been or will be—because
it is ours.

In this way, war is like love.)

∽

"The coffee is burnt."

"There's a draft."

"I can't bear the noise."

These are the sorts of excuses my father makes for
working at home, rather than in the café next door. I,
on the other hand, always find the coffee to be perfectly
palatable, the room warm, and beyond that, I've always
known my father to work best among cacophony—often
layering orchestral records atop the drumbeat of the
typewriter. It makes no sense that he would avoid the
place with such fervor. The only conclusion, then, is that
these excuses are lies.

This morning, my father seems particularly dis-
traught, and paces his study for hours. He is rabid with
new theories. Something about time and the ouroboros.
A war that I have never heard of, the name of which he
says again and again and again.

"It is the Second Eternity," he mutters. "It has all happened."

"What has happened?" I ask him.

My father's eyes are nearly lost in their sleepless sockets. "All that is to come."

⌇

Oral accounts from witnesses make up the entirety of our scholarly knowledge about the War of Fog. This, of course, is true for all wars and all times of peace alike. History is only history when experienced and subsequently reported. Our reality is nothing but what we perceive it to be. Nothing exists outside what is perceived.

And what did we who witnessed it perceive?

When the nine days' procession ended, the War of Fog simply began again.

⌇

It is raining. The creek is too high for wading. Oreno says that a collapsed bridge downstream made it rise like this—but when I tell Father, he only says that Oreno shouldn't be speaking of such things, and neither should I. I don't see why my father cares any which way for creeks and their depth, other than as an excuse to keep me quiet and indoors all day typing for him. I wish Oreno would come home from the war and do his job.

"So you miss me," Oreno prods, when I complain of his absence over supper. A smirk sits on his dopey, soft mouth.

"Of course I don't." The tips of my ears go hot. "I'm just tired of being my father's servant. You probably aren't any good at war, anyhow. You probably got scared at the first gunshot you heard and dropped your gun in the mustard fields."

"But you still want me to come back?" Oreno says, reaching for the cream.

"...yes."

"I'm sorry," he replies. "You will never see me again."

Unlike the other wars, there are no artifacts from the War of Fog. No bullets lodged in tree trunks so the bark swells around it like a tumor. No bayonets and no rifles. No helmets fractured by shrapnel. No casings nor cannons.

No bodies.

This is not because these elements were absent from the War of Fog. Rather, the opposite. Like the Army of Fog, the artifacts exist endlessly. They have neither entrance nor exit. This was the way of the First Eternity, and so too, it goes to reason, it is for the Second. If a thing exists forever, always beginning and happening and ending and beginning again, it both exists and does not exist. The Eternities Paradox thus makes it impossible for curators to gather and preserve, let alone exhibit, the artifacts from the War of Fog. How do you display an object that is at once premade and on a battlefield and eroded to dust? Even the famous blue-glass windows of Beldule are both taut in their frames and shattered from the fourth day of shelling. Sometimes, if you buy a fish at market and cut it open, you'll find a blue fragment the fish had gulped down in the creek. Such a find is considered lucky.

(Author's note: The Eternity Paradox is also what makes us, the survivors of the war, unable to ever know peace.)

I hate it here. I hate the cramped, dusty house that is always too hot. I hate the nail in the hall floorboard that never stays down no matter how many times Oreno hammers it, which has now ripped a hole in every pair of my stockings. I hate Oreno and the stupid way he rubs his hands over his belly when he is agitated, like he's trying to keep his insides from flopping out. I hate his eyelashes. I hate that he is here and I hate that he is not here and I hate that I mind either way. I hate the electric typewriter—especially the *F* and the *Y*, which always get jammed. I hate that I am rarely allowed outside anymore (Father says it isn't safe) and I hate my father's philosophies and his pipe smoke that wafts so constantly through the house that my hair smells like a city on fire. I hate his cough, which comes back every morning before we've had tea, and I hate his lies.

I will not say I hate my father. I know better than that. If I were to say that I hate him, something terrible would happen to him just to punish me.

∾

Let us return again to the Army of Fog. Or rather, not "return," as the Army of Fog has never left, but rolled onward and onward, uniforms blurring into a silver ribbon as they marched in formation.

I apologize. Language is inefficient in discussing the Army of Fog. Language is designed to be linear. To move a reader through time and story as if it were a road they, themselves, were marching down. Even the visual elements of language, as you can see, force the reader into a relationship with forward, linear progression. Your eyes move from left to right, one word at a time. In doing so, the reader, too, is dragged through time.

Sometimes I wonder whether these texts will be (are, have been) illegible. Will, now that the Second Eternity is at hand, reading even be possible? Without time, how can a time-dependent language exist? Perhaps we will all be rendered mute. And yet—the Army of Fog has begun singing as it marches.

One low lyric after the next.

⁓

Word comes that Oreno was killed in the war. I go to my father's study to break the news.

"See?" Oreno says. "I told you." He returns to his papers.

Oh, how humiliating, the tears that come then. I don't want Oreno to know I care that he's dead, so I run to the creek and I lay on the bank, looking up at the sky. I think of Oreno's face, its softness. Too soft for the war. Too soft for anything, really. I think how little I've grown to like him. Less and less each day. My heart, sharp as a piece of glass. Sharp as a needle. If only I could thread my heart, I would use it to stitch Oreno closed—there, at the gut, where a bayonet unpeeled him like a peach.

Birds fly overhead. Three crows, their open wings gleaming like arrowheads. I watch them for a long time, though they do not move—just remain suspended there, frozen mid-flight below the sun.

⁓

There was, despite the name, no fog in the War of Fog. The August in question was unseasonably clear. No dew pocked the late lilies, nor did a single cloud obscure the sky above Beldule.

When the uniformed troops, garbed in gray gabardine, marched in unbroken rows through the agricultural countryside, they appeared at a distance to be a single silver bank of fog.

    (Author's note: I have begun to question the necessity of my work. Without time, there can be no history. Without history, there is no need for a chronicler at all. If nothing can end, then what is the use of remembering it?)

I awaken in my own bed to find a weight on me. When I lift my arms, glass falls away like rain. The sound of chimes or broken windows. My room, full of blue glass. Spilling from the box. Pooled across the floor. It clusters like a heap of butterfly wings, jagged and bright. When I dig through the piles, I find only the same nine pieces, over and over, endlessly replicated. I catch my reflection in the mirror, and the mirror, too, is broken into nine pieces, one of me refracted in each slice, but each me is different from the last. Some of me are in my father's study. Some of me are here, in my bed, asleep. Some of me are hiding beneath the dining table. Some of me are with Oreno as he shows me exactly where the bayonet's blade went in. When I blink, I can see his liver, his kidney, his spleen—plump, wet jewels.

    Is this a dream?

The August in question was unseasonably clear.

Today is my birthday. I am fourteen years old! My father says that celebrating birthdays is foolish, because it's not like you wake up one morning as someone else—any more so than any other day of your life. But I *do* feel different. Not older, maybe, but more *precise* somehow. Like I'm one of my father's watches (the ones Oreno keeps wound and synched to the town clock) and someone has twisted a knob in me. Round and round the little gears turn, as if counting down the moments until—what? I don't even know. But I can feel it.

Despite my father's silly grudge against birthdays (and mirth in general), he does give me a present: a little music box holding a tiny automaton painter. The inside lid is mirrored, and I study my face in it for a long time, looking for signs of being fourteen.

I'll have to find something very special to keep in the box. My father tells me it belonged to my mother. He's also agreed (after ample begging) to buy me a raspberry cake. He's gone off to the café to fetch it, grumbling about frivolity, his pipe clenched between his teeth. I wonder if—

Oh, but there is some racket in the streets.

A great fog rises over the hill. :‖

DROWNING LESSONS

MY SISTER HAS DROWNED thirty-seven times. You might think that's impossible, but believe me, it's not. It's the truth. My sister has drowned in rivers, in bathtubs, and in soup bowls. She's drowned in swimming pools and drinking glasses. She has drowned in mall fountains and in sidewalk puddles and in the birdbath in the back garden—wherever she meets liquid, Sophia will find a way to drown. And I'm the guy with a lifetime's worth of lifeguard duty but no pay. You never really notice how much fluid there is around until you know someone who won't stop dying in it.

But listen—Sophia isn't the suicidal type. A lot of people think she is, but they're wrong. None of her drownings were on purpose. I know that seems hard to believe, given the thirty-seven overwhelming pieces of evidence to the contrary, but every single one has been accidental. Sophia isn't drawn to water; water is drawn to Sophia.

Take, for instance, when we went to the Renaissance fair and the Dunk-a-Peasant booth broke into a tidal wave right when Sophia walked by. Or when a fly ball at one of my baseball games knocked her unconscious, causing her to slump facedown into her neon-blue Slurpee. These things just happen to her.

Other times my sister will faint, unprovoked, and sink right into some new wet death. The worst is when she passes out in the shower and whoever finds her has to wrap her naked body up in a towel before reviving her. She doesn't look twenty years old when she's collapsed on the tile floor. She looks like a naked mole rat, or like a newborn snake, all slick and mushy.

Right now Sophia is on the sofa drinking whiskey out of a plastic sippy cup. Last March, a bottle's worth of wine burst out to reach her, and she had to get twelve stitches along her jaw from the glass shards. Since then, she can only drink out of "safe," nonbreakable cups—plus the cap keeps her mouth and nose protected from the contents as she swigs. It makes parties awkward; she looks like a toddler, suckling booze from a spill-proof lid. As my sister prefers to remain un-infantilized at social gatherings, she always pregames at home.

I melt into the couch next to her. She's watching some reality show about Catholic monks. The monks run a tattoo parlor and apiary. One of them is talking about how bees are nature's tattoo guns. He lifts up his robe to display a large orange honeycomb branded on his thigh, bordered with Latin script.

"I'm not so sure these monks are legit," I say.

"Mm." Her eyes remain on the monk, who is now leading the cameraman on a tour of the monastery. Bees waft past the lens in thin gray clouds. "Quinn's later?"

"You sure?" I ask. "Mom says it might rain."

"Whatever," she says. She takes in another sip of whiskey without flinching.

Sophia has not been particularly communicative as of late.

I leave her in the living room and head upstairs to get ready for Quinn's party.

∽

There is wanting and then there is *wanting*. It's ridiculous that the word *want* covers so much. Like, wanting a cool car is not the same thing as wanting Quinn. One of those is surface, material. The other kind of want is molecular. It's more like a tug. Like all these fishing lines are hooking into me and yanking. You can decide to want a car. You can't decide to want a person. Not in the same way. Like how Sophia couldn't decide whether to end up in Redland Pond this past September. The water just pulled and pulled and what could Sophia do but be dragged along? What can any of us do?

Wanting a car doesn't mess your whole digestive system up whenever you think about it. Doesn't make you so anxious (as you wriggle into your coat, as you button your jeans, as you imagine Quinn *un*buttoning your jeans, as you can almost feel her dusky burgundy lipstick smudging against your neck) that your whole body revolts in its own, tiny, raging war.

Maybe this is the difference between want and *yearn*: Want can be flipped on and off like a fuse. Want can be indulged in or set aside. Yearn is something else. You can hear it in the shape of the word. It sounds like the noise a person might make while lying on their stomach on the rim of a well, and reaching down into it, toward the dark. The little grunt they might emit as they reached and reached down into the belly of the well but never quite caught whatever it was they were reaching for.

∽

Sophia isn't allowed to drive anymore, so she rides shotgun. The last time my sister was allowed to operate a motor vehicle, she almost drove off a bridge before Mom grabbed the steering wheel. After that, our parents sold Sophia's car on Craigslist. We live in a small town, no public transit or anything, so she's pretty much stuck at home unless I lug her out with me.

Creature. That's what I named the beat-up Volvo I bought this past June. A seventeenth-birthday present to myself, paid for in long-hoarded bar mitzvah money. In AP US History, I learned that the Puritans used to name their daughters things like Creature and Fear, and their boys Truelove. I like the idea of girls with monstrous names. I also like the idea of cars named after girls named after monsters. Sophia thinks it's a stupid name for a car, but she doesn't get a say in it. I'm the one doing her the favor of driving her around all the time.

Sophia was supposed to leave for college this fall. She took a year off post high school (a "gahhp yahh" she'd yawn in a faux British accent—back when she still made jokes)—and then got into UVM, a few hours' drive away. I think she was ready to be somewhere new, somewhere she could walk down the street without every passerby knowing her as "that drowning girl."

But then, the week before she was due to leave, a kid found her facedown in Redland Pond.

Usually it takes only a few minutes to revive Sophia—we've all gotten pretty damn efficient at it—but this time, she didn't come back for almost an hour. Once she did wake up, she stayed loopy and confused for the next few days. She snapped out of it before the week was up, but our parents decided that letting her go off to school alone was too much of a risk. They made her un-enroll. Since then, Sophia has spent most of her time pissed off and watching reality TV, which she has deemed the only stimulus worthy of her attention.

✒

It's already well past dark. Quinn lives about fifteen minutes outside town, on a dirt road. Her parents are both lawyers, and they have this big mansion in the woods, plus another place in New York. Most of the time, Quinn's rich parents are working in the city, and Quinn is left behind to go to school and watch the house. She's an only child. That must be how her parents stay rich—not spending all their money on college enrollments and ER visits and military-grade life jackets.

That's another thing—our parents make Sophia wear this puffy red life jacket everywhere. I mean *everywhere*. If they catch her without it on, even in the house, even in *bed*, they give her this big lecture about responsibility and common sense. She's sewed all these band patches and stuff on it and had some of her friends sign it the way you get people to sign a cast, but it still looks . . . well, ridiculous. Though, I mean, I want her to wear it, too. I don't want her to die.

All the people who signed Sophia's vest are off at college now. Only their scribbles left behind. Scribbles—and Sophia.

We round Slate Street, past the rows of looming green-gray buildings that were once a button factory. They're all empty now. So much of this town is more "what was" than "what is." Abandoned factories, junked car lots, bridges too rickety to bear weight anymore. We don't cross bridges anyway, though, not with Sophia in the car. We always take a detour.

∽

The driveway at Quinn's is packed, so we park down the road by the woods and walk the rest of the way. Overhead, clouds gather, heavy and electric. A lick of anticipation dangling in the air. At the end of the cul-de-sac, the pale glow of the party leaks out into the night. Bass buzzes across the front porch. A few kids lag on the stoop, smoking American Spirits and passing a joint around. I squint to see if Quinn is among them. She isn't.

"How much cash do you think I can scam off these idiots?"

"Huh?"

That's the first full sentence Sophia has spoken to me in three days. She tacks a dollar bill to her life jacket with a safety pin.

"Come on, Dalton, haven't you heard that it's *good luck* to pin a dollar on someone who's come back from the dead?" She winks at me.

"You're an asshole," I reply. She bats her eyelashes.

"I heard that if you make it ten bucks, you're guaranteed ten years of great sex."

I ignore her.

"Come on," she nudges. "If you help me spread the rumor, I'll give you twenty-five percent."

"Fifty percent," I say.

"Forty."

I sigh. "Deal."

We get to the front door, pushing past the smokers and into the foyer. I glance around for Quinn—still no sign of her. Already, Sophia's darted off to make her fortune. There was a time when conversations used to snuff out as she passed through a room, eyes flicking toward her in morbid curiosity. But novelty wears off fast in a town this small. Once people figure you out, they stop caring. She's like a mascot. All people see is this familiar cartoon outline of a person, completely ignoring the actual person inside.

I approach the one group of kids who are all staring at my sister, whispering to one another. I don't know any of them, but one's wearing a Leland and Gray homecoming pin, which is the high school two towns over. Fresh blood.

"Hey," I say. "You know it's good luck to pin a dollar to her life jacket. It'll help you get laid, or whatever."

"Bullshit," says a girl with dyed powder-pink hair and a torn pair of fishnets over her arms.

"Believe what you want," I say, "but it's worth a try, right?"

The pink girl hesitates. One of her friends, a punk with thick black eyeliner applied a little too cleanly under each eye reaches into his pocket. Gropes around for a dollar. I leave. Game, set, match. At least this way, there'll always be people near Sophia. To keep an eye on her. Just in case.

I work my way toward the back of the foyer. It's a huge, round room with a crystal chandelier dangling from the lofted ceiling. Ten or twelve looming paintings hang down the full length of the walls. They're all primed white canvases with a single, measured green stripe running from top to bottom. I asked Quinn about them once, and she said her artist uncle painted them, that they were supposed to be blades of grass, up close. Standing in the center of the room, you feel like an ant—a minuscule creature looking up at the looming grasses, the vaulted ceilings, the walls that go up and up and up, the chandelier shivering with gold light like the sun in late autumn. It's like that movie *Honey, I Shrunk the Kids*, where Rick Moranis almost murders his children with utter laboratory negligence, but they get to eat a giant candy bar, so it's all worth it.

I don't like feeling small like that.

"But that's the *point*," Quinn had insisted.

Imagine being so rich that feeling insignificant was an *aesthetic novelty*. A sensation so foreign, you experimented with it in your interior design. Just for kicks.

I make my way up the staircase, which lies curled in the back of the room like a ringlet of dark hair. The mahogany balustrade is waxed and polished enough to see your reflection in the wood. It reminds me of water. I keep my hands off it.

The first time I kissed Quinn, we were drunk, in the woods behind our friend Carl's house. Carl had stolen a bottle of rum from his parents' liquor cabinet and we'd finished the whole thing between the three of us. It was late December. The trees were skeletal, the ground frozen and crusted with ice. I don't remember how it started—the world was hazy, smudged out of focus by the rum, time wiggling back and forth. But I remember the taste of Quinn's mouth, like woodsmoke and honey, and I remember her weight over me, pressing me into the forest floor. I remember thinking about the root system beneath us, tangling in a thousand hidden capillaries under the soil, and how the leafless branches above us looked like veins, too, and how I could feel the blood moving in my own body, like my pulse and the sky and the ground were all the same thing. And I was going to say this to Quinn, but then she kissed my neck, so all I said instead was "You're kissing my neck!" which I think I said aloud as a sort of proof. A verification that it was all really happening.

☙

There's a clump of kids at the top of the stairs, playing Arnold Arnold. It's a drinking game local to our high school—invented by a kid who graduated six or seven years ago, first name Arnold, last name Arnold. I try to press through but someone grabs my arm.

"Dalt, will you play corner? We need a fourth." It's Maritime Levine, a girl infamous for ripping another girl's hoop earring out during a cafeteria brawl. She's a psycho, but we're kind of friends. We sit next to each other in French class. I try to shrug past, looking for Quinn down the corridor toward her room, but Maritime pushes a lukewarm can of PBR at me. There are two other players—Maritime's best friend Ximena (the other half of the Great Hoop Earring Fiasco) and Graham Fell-ing, a theater kid who was obviously roped in against his will. Her grip on my arm tightens. "We're three checks in, Beloveds round."

Arnold Arnold is played in five rounds, or "checks": Strangers, Friends, Beloveds, Graveyard, and Thieves, each with their own set of tasks or dares, which get progressively weirder the deeper into the game you get.

"You wanna start, cutie?" Maritime asks me.

"Sure. Ximena?" I put out my hand, palm up. "Do the honors?" She spits into it. It's strangely cold, like she's been chewing on an ice cube. Then she puts her hand out and I do the same. We clasp them together. We'll have to keep our hands like this until the final round. At the end, we'll each try to get someone at the party to high-five our spit hand. Whoever gets high-fived first wins the round. The loser drinks. It isn't the most refined game on the planet.

When we get to Graveyard, Maritime pulls a lighter out of her pocket and flicks the flame alive. It glints off the ruby acrylic of her nails.

"Burn for three," she says, turning to Graham. His eyes go wide and he shakes his head.

"Drink," he says, and takes a swig of his beer.

"Coward," Maritime scoffs.

"I'll do it." Sophia's appeared next to Ximena, sidling into the circle without invitation. She holds out a closed fist.

Maritime raises an eyebrow, but holds the fire up to my sister's skin. It slithers along her knuckles, leaving a black, sooty streak. "One. Two. Three." She doesn't twitch. It creeps people out, whenever Sophia plays the Graveyard round. She really acts like she doesn't feel . . . well, *anything.*

"Okayyy . . ." Ximena frowns. "So are you, like, joining the game? 'Cause we already have evens." She stares my sister down, lips pursed.

Sophia shrugs, taking the hint as she gets back up from the circle. I look at the floor. "Dalton can have my Drink bonus." She winks at me. "Just keeping an eye on you, sweet pea." Then she turns, vanishing back into the fray.

⁓

Once, Sophia was interviewed for an online paranormal investigations magazine called *Otherwhere!* I'm not sure how they found out about her, but they sent two reporters over to talk to her. Why they couldn't have sent the questions through email is beyond me, but I guess they wanted to *witness* her in person. I remember one of the guys looked super bro-y, wearing a salmon-pink polo shirt and a backward Red Sox cap, which I'll admit, I didn't expect. The other had on a baggy blue T-shirt that read DO YOU KNOW WHERE YOUR KRAKEN IS?, which, okay, I did expect. They asked her all these questions about being dead, about what she'd seen in those moments before she'd come back.

Halfway into the interview, she told them this story: Our parents took us to the beach in Maine one summer. She was seven and I was four. This was before the drownings started. She'd been playing at the shore and got tugged under a wave. It swallowed her, this leviathan wall of water with her tiny body tucked inside it. She tossed and gulped and paddled, and at last managed to get out and drag herself ashore. But while she was being thrown against the surf, her foot was sliced open, and a fragment of purple wampum shell had lodged itself in her heel. Our mom had tried to fish it out with tweezers, but couldn't get to it, so the wound healed over with the shard still inside. *And ever since . . .* (Sophia leaned in close to the microphone, her voice lowering into a near-growl, the interviewers' eyes swelling like flying saucers) . . . *that shell has been trying to get back to the ocean. Pulling me back with it.*

None of that shit ever happened. We never went to the beach as kids. Not once. It would have been nice if the story were true. What I mean is, it's nice when things have a reason for happening. When a diagnosis has an explanation attached. Cause and effect. Because if you know the *why* of a malady, you can take steps toward fixing it. But the fact of it is, we don't know why this is happening. She drowns and drowns and drowns and there's no point in any of it.

She lies all the time, these days. I think at a certain point, it just seemed easier that way—after all her friends left town and she realized she wasn't going anywhere for what could be a long, long time. If nobody really knows you, then no one knows if you're telling the truth. And if no one knows if you're telling the truth, you can decide what the truth is, and what it isn't. You have the control. Even when the water is rising.

∽

"Copycat?" Maritime asks, already moving on. She offers the lighter up to Ximena.

"Copycat," Ximena agrees, and Maritime holds the flame under her friend's palm, *one, two three*. Ximena hisses.

"My turn," she says. She shifts toward me, then slips her hand up under my shirt. It's still hot from the lighter. I shiver. She starts to trail her fingers down my stomach when I see Quinn at the end of the far hall, emerging from her bedroom. She sees me, too. I jerk Ximena away.

"I'm out, I—uh, sorry." I duck away from the game.

"You have to drink!" Maritime calls after me as I leave, following Quinn down the hall. On the landing below, I can see Sophia float by the edge of the room. She's alone, a bouquet of dollar bills clotted to her chest. She leans against the wall beside a green painting and stares into the mass of people. Or maybe beyond them—out the window, where wind knits through the creaking sycamores. She doesn't have any friends at this party. She doesn't have any friends in this whole town anymore. A low roll of thunder hums over the house, and Sophia's eyes go glassy. But no rain yet. As long as there's no rain . . .

I turn back to the second-floor hall. The corridor is thick with more party guests, and Quinn hovers at the far end by the entrance to her room, a thin silver flask in one hand. She's wearing a long pink jumpsuit with black polka dots, the kind I'm not sure how girls get in and out of. Like maybe they have to be born in a jumpsuit and slowly grow into it with age, like the reverse of a snail growing out of its shell. Quinn's cropped, iron-straight hair levitates just over her shoulders. Not a single strand out of place. I once heard you can tell rich people from normal people by how well taken care of their hair looks. I squeeze through the crowd to get closer to her.

"Ey, Dalt!" Carl slaps me on the chest, diving in front of me. He's built like a bureau, looming and thick, even one of his shoulders meaty enough to block the whole hall from view. When I crane around him, Quinn's gone. Carl offers me a swig of gin, but I've already pushed past him and am making my way toward the bedroom. Through the open door I think I see Quinn's reflection glide across a mirror—but when I get into the room, she isn't there.

Everything in her bedroom is the same as it was last time I was here: the red-and-white pelican quilt pinned to the ceiling, the row of little gold bottles holding dried roses, the velvet love seat with a wine stain on the arm. I can almost see shadows of the two of us on the cushions, or leafing through the bookshelf, or lifting the needle on the record player. All these versions of ourselves from past days, still imprinted on the space.

I pluck up a silk ribbon, spilled in a coil on the floor. Run it through my hands. A strand of Quinn's hair shakes loose. When I look up, she's standing in the doorway.

"I, uh, I didn't know you were coming," she says. I shrug. Her hands vanish into her jumpsuit pockets. Poof, a disappearing act.

"Oh—yeah. Here I am. I mean, is that okay? I guess I thought—"

"No, it's fine. You're totally welcome."

"Thanks. I mean—yeah, thanks." I realize I'm still holding the ribbon. I've wrapped it around my thumb tight enough that my skin has turned purple. Quinn glances at it.

"Look, can I talk to you for a second?" My voice doesn't sound like my voice. It sounds like it's coming from someone else, and I'm standing a few feet away, eavesdropping.

She nods. She doesn't move to close the door.

"I haven't heard from you in a while," I say. My eyes keep drifting off to the side to watch all the little shadows of past-us move around, making out in the corner, tying up their boots, eating fried chicken in bed off greasy paper plates.

"I've been really busy," she says. She doesn't elaborate.

"Okay, yeah, me too. Super busy."

"You've been okay, though?" she asks.

"Yeah, totally. Busy. And good."

"Good," she says. We stand there quiet. Another buzz of thunder passes over the house.

"Listen, Quinn—" I take a step toward her. My pulse thuds against my throat, like some tiny me inside the bigger me is banging on a door, begging to be let the fuck out so it can get out of Dodge before whatever happens next happens.

I reach up. Touch her arm. I can feel her skin, cool, through the sleeve of her jumpsuit. "I miss you."

Her eyes fall to the floor.

I wonder if she can sense my heartbeat through my fingertips. Morse code. SOS.

"I'm sorry, Dalton . . ." She pulls away.

∽

When a person drowns, it's because the body calls for something it can't have. That is to say, your body demands that you breathe, even when no oxygen is available. Holding your breath is a conscious choice. The longer you hold it, the higher the carbon dioxide levels in your blood rise, and the desire to breathe intensifies. The desire mounts and mounts until eventually, the desire is so irresistible that you willingly allow water down your airway and into your lungs. You choose this. Every cell in your body insists, *This. This is what you need.* There is wanting and there is yearning—and then, there is a lung filling with water.

∾

A flash of light shudders through the room, and a few moments later thunder cracks so loud the whole house shakes. I can hear it on the roof: sheets of water aching down from the split lip of the sky, all at once. *Rain.*

"I have to go," I blurt. I sprint past Quinn, down the hall, down the spiral staircase, through the throngs of kids in the foyer. I can't find Sophia. I call her name, but my voice is swallowed by music and laughter. I call out again anyway. Carl, giant that he is, looms above the crowd by the entrance to the kitchen. I weave through the bodies toward him, through people dancing, couples kissing each other in the dark.

"Hey man, have you seen my sister?" My heart is beating so hard that my shoulders shake with each pulse.

"Yeah, dude, I think she stepped out for a smoke. Like ten minutes ago, I dunno."

I run. The rain is too loud. Louder than it should be. I've never heard a sound that loud. The rest of the party doesn't seem to notice. How can they not notice?

As I round the corner, the edge of the counter jams into my side. My breath cannonballs out of me. I keep running. Past the dining room, through the mudroom, out the back door.

"Sophia!" I yell into the storm.

"*Damn*, Dalt, what?"

She's sitting on the covered back porch, the tangerine pupil of her cigarette glowing in the dusk. Dry as toast. I let my panic flow out, like I'm draining a tub. There's a broken lawn chair next to her and I slide into it.

"Hey." I catch my breath. "The rain's pretty when it doesn't try to fucking kill you, huh?" I side-eye her. Normally, that's the sort of remark that would get her to smirk. But she isn't smiling.

"Dollar for your thoughts?" I nod at the clump of money on her vest.

She takes another couple drags of the cigarette, tosses the butt in a puddle.

"Remember that road trip I took out west for Sara and Marie's wedding? Like, three summers ago?" she asks.

"Sure, yeah, you and Bo drove out, I remember."

She dips a toe out into the rain, pulls it back. "We stopped at this museum sort of place, somewhere in New Mexico. Like, an oddities cabinet. Fetuses in jars, Fiji mermaids, that sort of crap. Hoax stuff. Their main display was called the Arctic Woman. They claimed it was like two thousand years old. They kept it in a separate room, where you couldn't take pictures, and you had to pay an extra few bucks to get in. In the middle of the room was this big coffin thing, a huge box, with a spotlight on it. And when you go up, you realize it's a freezer. There's this woman in there, suspended in a block of ice. Dead or whatever . . . I don't even know if it's legal. But man, all day, people come to stare at this girl. People stumbling in off the highway, looking for something to kill time, looking for something different. And she's stuck in this fucking ice. Jammed in there, a human Popsicle. Where no one can get to her. They can see her. But they can't get to her."

Sophia reaches to grab another cigarette, but the carton is empty.

"I was just thinking about that . . ." she says.

I pull a crumpled dollar out of my pocket and pin it to her vest.

"Let's get out of here," I say. "This party sucks. Hang here, I'll grab my coat."

I duck back inside, shoving past a kid puking in the sink. Glancing up the stairs, I can spot Quinn again, talking to a guy I don't know. She leans close. Mutters into his ear. Untangling my jacket from the pile in the hall, I sling my coat over my shoulder and head back toward the porch. When I return—Sophia isn't there.

In the distance, just outside the lights of the party, a dark shape is silhouetted against the sky. A girl's body, swaying back and forth, arms at her sides. She's standing on her toes, but it looks unnatural, like a ballerina on pointe. As if the clouds have grabbed hold of her, are forcing her upward. As I get closer, I can see her face— upturned to the sky. Her eyelids are peeled back, her eyes transformed into black lakes. The rain falls directly into them but she doesn't blink, doesn't move. My sister's mouth is craned wide open and full of water. She looks like a park fountain, water up to the brim of her lips, head yanked back, a stream of rain pouring out. I'm only a few feet away now, and it seems like more water is pouring *out* of her mouth than *into* it. How can that be? She leans into the wind like a sapling.

As I get to her, she falls. I hear a snap, and I can't tell if she landed on a stick or it came from her ankles. Water still rises from her mouth, streams out her nose and ears. I do what I can to cover her with my body, to shield her from the rain.

This is the part I know well. Push on the center of the chest. Hard and fast, twice per second. Repeat thirty times, then administer rescue breaths. I tip her onto her side so the last of the water leaves her, then put my mouth on hers. One. Two. I pump my own breath into her. The sky blooms again with light. Back to her chest. Twenty-eight, twenty-nine, thirty. Damp bills tear off under my hands. Two more breaths. *Please, come on.*

She coughs. A gush rivers out of her, and then, she's crying. She's back. I smear the hair out of her face. She looks up at me, mascara carving down her cheeks in dark ravines. She tries to say something, but her voice is too quiet and ragged to hear. I lean in.

"It . . . it happened again?"

"Yeah," I say. "Yeah. It happened again."

"Nobody saw . . . did they?"

Behind us, the party writhes on. The lights bright, the music cutting out through the storm. I should have stayed closer. I shouldn't have left her alone. If Sophia's friends had been in town, they would have followed her out. She never would have made it into the rain. Or no, she would never have been here at all, at this stupid high school party, alone. She would never have passed through the throngs like a ghost, unnoticed, untouched, never would have wandered invisibly out the back door and into the storm. This party she wasn't even invited to, that her little brother dragged her to because he felt sorry for her. She wouldn't have had to die, alone in a storm. Again.

"No," I tell her. "No. Nobody saw."

THE AUTUMN KILL

THE HUNTER'S MOON IS come. It is time to cull meat from the woodlands. I will shuck flesh like corn husks. I will snap open a living belly like a pocket watch. I know rabbits will hide anywhere—in a coin purse; down wells; tucked into their own mouths. Deer flirt with invisibility. They weave yarn through their antlers, blanket themselves in wren feathers and branches. What a waste. What a fool's sport. I carry home their bodies in a cotton sack. Warthogs do not hide, but bullet toward me, stinking of clumsiness. I pirouette once and tusks shed. Twice, and skeleton whips loose from muscle. Thrice, and lungs silence like drumskin, smothered.

I was killed once, too—swept from my mother's bed and carved into a huntress. My neighbors sharpened my hands into bayonets. Turned my hip to dagger sheath. My teeth, they filed down to points. They made me chant the song a spine sings when it breaks. Little lullaby. Then they married me to the Hunter's Moon, and I wore a dog-jaw crown. I braided sinew into my hair. Our wedding bed was built of talons and blood and grease. *We are hungry, o huntress,* my neighbors said. *The fury is sweet in you now. It will choke many elk to their knees. It will fatten us through winter.*

I give them the bounty for which they beg. There is death in the mirror. Meat hangs salted in the stockroom. October swells ripe like a blackberry on the briar. Gold filigree has etched the trees with light.

∽

Before the Marriage, I was a girl, like you. What, you think this impossible? You think huntresses are one sort and you, something completely different? I understand why you would think that way. It's easier.

I worked at the gas station off exit 12. Truckers came for lottery tickets, for gasoline, for bags of roasted cashews and Twix bars. There was a kitchen in the back, where the man who owned the gas station cooked jerk goat in Caribbean spices each night for five dollars a plate. I was the cashier, opening and closing the register in thousands of small chimes and rattles. I cannot remember much from those days, but I remember the chime. So many small bells churning in the machine. The perfume of ginger and nutmeg simmering. The young men who came in for malt liquor, for three-dollar bottles of Merlot, for bright aluminum cans of beer. Heat rising from their male bodies in midsummer. I think I wanted something of them. I cannot remember what I wanted. All that was before. When food was plentiful. When the skies were bright. When I was still a mortal thing.

⌒

This is how to field dress and butcher a snowshoe hare: First, cut off the head with a sharp edge—a glass fragment from a shattered window; a jag of a torn tin can. Then, remove the four feet so the dead hare cannot run. Slip a finger beneath the skin and loosen it. Curl hide away from muscle like an orange peel. Night will slip in. Your own breath will enter as a ghost. Slice down the skin with the razor point of your index finger. Yank the body out of its fur. When free from its coat, the hare will try to flee. Its head will reach for its body. Its tendons will thrill with motion. Seize it with your teeth, the strongest part of you. Hum low tunes until it stills—songs of burnt sugar, of wheat fields buzzing with locusts. When the dead hare calms, make a small incision in the stomach and reach inside. Pull out what lies there: intestines, liver, bicycle gears, sheet music to violin songs no one plays anymore. Leave its heart. All meat is sweeter with the heart still in it. Or so I am told by those who eat this bounty. I do not eat anymore. I do not need to.

⌒

Please shut up about the end of the world. Yes, the world changed. It does not matter how or when. All worlds end, at some point, and new ones sprout from them. There is always a war to slough off our father's names. A rainfall of bombs to plant as seedlings in our kitchens, in our scalps. Call this new world a sapling. Call me the bough stretching out from a newborn tree. No more chimes. The planet has shrunk down. Lost its ties to itself. We use the debris of our old lives as weapons. Everything can be a weapon, if held skillfully. The old gods died when the red snow fell. Now the people have new gods: A moon that swells until she almost rots, then retreats into mourning. A famine. The beasts that feed the famine. The girl who slaughters the beasts.

∽

I can see by the way you hold your shoulders that you fear me. Did you know humans instinctively lift their shoulders to their ears when in danger? This is to protect the neck, the most vulnerable part of the body. For a while, humans removed themselves from the food chain, but the body never knew this. The body is blind to time. It continues its same old dance. Instead of lifting the shoulders to keep the jugular hidden from a wildcat's bite, the shoulders would rise in heavy traffic, when a meeting ran late, before a blind date. Little annoyances or anxieties that the body mistook for peril. Now the true dangers have returned to us and the body can do what it was built for. See? You can feel your pulse throb against your collarbone. How your throat is tucked so safely away. In this feral age, our bodies are working properly again. Our instincts are no longer wasted.

You are wise to be afraid.

∽

An efficient predator must think like her prey, so she may always be one step ahead. For the hunted, *one step ahead* is death. So the best hunters must be already dead.

∽

I think I had a chime in my chest once. How it rang and rang and would not stop ringing. When blood moved through me, the bell's clapper waved it past. There were times when the chime called out in strange, ugly pangs, but not because of the blood. I cannot remember what made the chime call out. A certain swelling, like a sickness, where the chime would grow so loud I could hardly breathe. I am lucky the chime has gone quiet now. The ringing was unbearable. I am lucky.

∽

Other dead cities have created creatures like myself. Have conducted similar ceremonies of cleaver and blood. Once, as I stalked a young black bear through the sycamore grove, I glimpsed another of my kind. She was climbing one of the old trees with astonishing speed, and when I grew close, I saw that her hands had been replaced with jagged steel hooks. On another dusk, I met a huntress at the riverbed whose fingers and toes had been sewn together with fishing wire. Slick paddles for diving into the trout waters. On another still, I glimpsed hovering near the honeybees—her jaw had been removed, and bees wafted in and out of her throat, which filled to the brim with nectar for her neighbors to harvest.

∽

You know why our neighbors brought you here, yes? Why they have trapped you here, with me? Of course you do. You felt the earth tilt toward autumn. You have endured the same hunger pangs we have all endured, as if the whole long-dead city shares a single belly, starving in tandem. Children have been born in the turning year, and not enough of them died in the cradle. There are new hungers to sate. More hunger than I alone can kill.

I know, I know—you are just a girl.

So was I.

Were you married already, in the world before this one? No, of course not, you are too young. Then the ceremony tonight will be your first. I suppose you never died before, either. No matter, it is an easy trick to learn. All you have to do is study the way a goat's eyes darken when a blade glides over its throat. Follow its lead.

Once, I came upon a farmhouse just before dawn. The owners had fled or been eaten by their own hogs. By some providence, the horses had survived, alone in the stables. They had learned to lift the little latch between the stable and the hayloft, and had been eating rations of hay, but the hay had run out. And so, the stallions killed and ate the weakest of their own herd.

All creatures will become hunters, if they must.

The horses had done what they had to do for survival. They learned skills uncommon for a beast of burden, had transcended their species' limits. But no matter—I led them back to the village, where I butchered them and cut their meat into strips and tanned their hides, and my neighbors feasted for days.

All creatures become prey when the time is right.

Some of these trees are thousands of years old. Can you imagine? To be a sequoia in an old-growth forest, let to live and live and live and keep on living. Let to reach so far toward the sky, lesser beings can hardly see the top of you. And as your body grows, you become a home: termites and weevils, owls tending to their downy young, webbed pouches of hatching moths, squirrels fattening in a hollowed branch. Your body, a city. Your body, sustaining and feeding and sheltering so many—and all the while, you never have to die. You never have to kill.

$$\backsim$$

The time has come to cull meat from the woodlands.

I lift my knife to you, and what do you say? Do you thank me? Do you shiver like a leaf in wind?

Look at my hands—they are weapons. Look at my teeth, my breasts, my hips . . . Every part of me is designed for the slaughter. You are still soft. You are still a living thing. Your ghost is still stitched to your flesh. Mine? My ghost tumbled out of me many years ago. Sometimes I pass it in the forest, mistaking it for a pheasant, and try to shoot it down.

The neighbors want a second huntress.

But I will not make one.

Go. Follow the moonlight away from here. Follow the creek bed, filling with blood. Follow the silver slug trails over moss beds. Follow the thunder of bombs, and then turn away. Find some other place than this. If there is the hunter, and the hunted, there must be a third creature— one between. The sequoia, who is neither. The creek bed, who is neither. The stars, ringing their endless distant chimes. Find the stars and ring them for me. I would tell you to sing my name, if I could remember it.

Yes, the neighbors—they will be angry. But what can they do to me for freeing you? Kill me? They cannot kill me. I am death.

FIFTY BEASTS
TO BREAK YOUR HEART

INTRODUCTION:

WE'LL ADMIT—THE EDITORS OF *this bestiary are not zoologists. We did consult a PhD in animal sciences, but she didn't do any real work. We only hired her to appear more credible to the scientific community. The rest of us are florists. This makes us more qualified to conduct this research than just about anyone else. We spend all day touching beautiful things (both edible and poisonous), so we are experts when it comes to monsters. Monsters and flowers aren't much different. Sometimes they are hard to tell apart—but a good florist knows what to look for.*

Our customers rely on us to ease apologies (tulips; marigold; a single lily), to ensure everlasting affection (baby's breath, red carnation), to see a beloved into the next life (orchid and rose). We bear a responsibility to convey our clients' passions with accuracy. But what to do when primrose is not enough? When the greenhouse can no longer contain a client's longing? Then—a bolder bouquet is needed.

A rose can say a lot, but a Yslani can say more. Why give a hyacinth when you could offer your beloved a Finlir, shaking on its knees?

Through fieldwork, ethnographic study, and somber reflection, we set out to prove that anything could, in the hands of a skilled florist and in a vase of the right size, become a bouquet.

(We have since learned that it is possible to learn too much.)

What follows is a compendium of regional creatures, studied and cataloged in the order in which we encountered them. We conducted this labor over the course of many months, and it cannot be said this time passed without significant setbacks. Still, we believe our report to be of value to any dedicated craftsman of the floral arts, as well as to the occasional interested outsider.

Do not be thrown by the many rumors in this text. There is much we cannot say for sure—unsubstantiated facts. What is true will not cleanly be separated from superstition. The truth is none of your business.

If you are not a florist but stubborn enough to read this anyway, here's a test:

What is your favorite flower?

If you answered with anything other than a creature listed in this book, you'd be smart to revise your answer before they find out. The beasts here are a vain lot.

———————

Here are a few more test questions:

> What is the most hideous thing you ever
>   nurtured?
> What shape is a phantom limb?
> What wine pairs best with the most lonesome
>   meal?
> What is enough?

Again, if you did not answer with one of the beasts in this text, you are only putting yourself at risk. We're telling you this as friends. If this document acts as anything, let it be a map of hunger. Let it be flint. Let it be a warning.

Signed,

Dr. Larkspur, researcher
Dr. Ghost Pipe, researcher
Dr. Phlox, floricultural illustrator

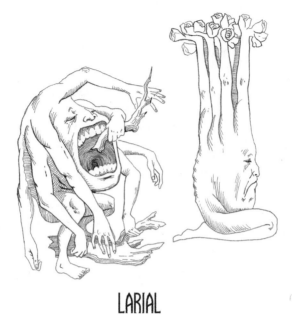

LARIAL

The Larial was not always so hungry. Old lore says the first Larial awoke to find it had eaten its lover in the night, and it has been ravenous ever since. When the Larial feeds, it unbuckles the leather belt keeping its jaw closed. Its mouth falls slack and its seven arms fill the mouth with crop. The Larial eats anything earthen. It strips boughs from sycamore, devours river stones and soil, and swallows deer skeletons abandoned on the forest floor. Its appetite bores holes through mountains and empties lakes. Once the Larial has eaten its fill, it holds its seven hands to the sun and waits. Soon, the rain will come. Soon, the hands will sprout alive. When they do, wildflowers bound up from the flesh, and the seven hands become gardens.

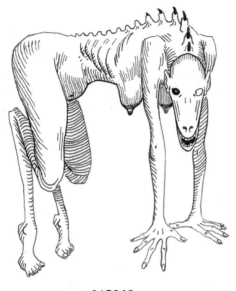

SORBIS

At the edge of town, where Chestnut Street bisects Ghost Water Boulevard, lies a crossroads. The air is hazed with wood pulp turned smoke, swept up by eastern winds passing the paper mill. A rumor states that if you wait there for the devil, you can trade your soul in exchange for otherworldly guitar chops or a booming dentistry career or a lifelong tropical vacation. Those down-and-out enough are prone to superstition. They'll believe just about anything. They'll even believe that your average Sorbis is Satan himself.

The Sorbis' burrow lies just beneath the spot where the four streets converge. The Sorbis is pink like a hairless cat or a plucked chicken, and has a long, narrow snout and a spiked spine. One of its eyes is charcoal, the other icy blue. Some poor sap mistaking it for the devil will be fool enough to look into the blue eye. Stare too long, and she's prone to start seeing impossible things. She'll see the board members of the King Poppy

Floral Convention falling to their knees in awe at her and her colleagues' immense and invaluable contributions. She'll see them crowd into her flower shop and buy peony after peony, just to give them back to her in amorous fistfuls. She'll see Ghost Pipe come home, unscathed. His hands: speckled with ink and missing no fingers. Even after she leaves the crossroads, after she leaves the Sorbis and its eye and the flower shop and the town behind, she'll keep seeing these things—reflecting in every shop window, every lake face, every mirror, shuddering against the cinema of the sky.

DYRN

Few have seen the Dyrn coatless. Wrapped in many furs, it does not know cold, nor wind, nor touch. Like a rose, the Dyrn is built of layers that, when peeled away, reveal the true beast. One coat is bearskin. Another is goose down. Deeper still, there is a birch-bark coat and a coat of eyelashes and another of sea foam. At the center, once all the layers have unfurled, is nothing but a single tooth. A Dyrn tooth is considered most lucky in the pocket—to those hunters cruel enough to reveal it.

GETLY

The Getly sings, and its prey listens. Oh, what a sound, how riotous and sweet. The prey's heart is a rattle seized to shake. *Don't stop singing,* begs the prey, leaning closer to the Getly's open mouth. *Don't stop singing.* The Getly obliges, and the prey climbs into the Getly's throat. The Getly sings until the prey has forgotten its own name. It sings of highways and shipyards, of hotel rooms and riverbeds. It keeps singing until the prey has slipped into its belly and dissolved, no longer a living thing but merely food: fuel for a song.

CORVOST

The Corvost is a crow-like bird, but instead of feathers, the Corvost is armored in hundreds of coins, flattened by locomotives. While still in the nest, mother Corvosts snatch pennies from sidewalks and pockets. They lay this bounty along train rails like rows of pearls, waiting to be pressed. Later, they collect the smothered coins and return to the nest. When their eggs hatch, it is on a bed of these treasures, and as the fledglings grow, the coins fuse to them. By the time they are large enough to leave the nest, they have become entirely feathered in copper.

Larkspur soaked a Corvost feather overnight in a cup of Coke and found it to shine up nicely. Ghost Pipe disagreed with this method, preferring the natural tarnish of time. Thus, in Phlox's rendering, he tried to depict the Corvost diplomatically. Corvosts would pair nicely with purple heather as a hostess gift.

(Editors' note: We do not actually have botanical names. That would be excruciatingly pat. We use these pen names not for our safety, but for yours.)

PLUVIUS

Very few believe that the Pluvius is alive. How can it be? Where is its heart, its liver, its lung? How does it eat? Where are the others? Isn't it only a thin mist hovering over a high school parking lot? Well, as any good florist can tell you, this is both true and dangerously untrue, so be careful whom you ask.

TINSE

In the old country, sheep went missing from pastures when the harvest was high. Bones were found at the forest's edge the next morning. Everyone assumed it was wolves. Most people still do.

The only record of the truth came from one local farmer, who encountered a Tinse on his way home from the pharmacy. He told the whole town what he'd seen: a ram-horned monster with a broad chest, and fitted into the center of the chest was a door, and fitted into the left side of the door, over the monster's heart, was a knob. The farmer saw the beast turn the doorknob and saw the ribs swing open. The monster bowed to its knees in the meadow, and a flock of sheep wandered in, one by one, vanishing into the mansion of the Tinse's body.

The townspeople didn't believe the farmer. They ridiculed

him. Called him mad. No one would buy his milk or meat. His crop went sick. A year later, he wandered into the woods and found the Tinse breathing against the dusk, the door hanging open on its hinges—an invitation.

(Did Ghost Pipe follow?)

SERRIN

Lift up the ocean like a rug. Beat it with a broom handle. Algae and salt will scatter in place of cobwebs, but the effect is the same. Do a thorough job and the Serrin will thank you for it. Serrin prefer a clean house. They are in the habit of sweeping the water's surface clear of ships. Behind every squall and every widow is a Serrin tidying up. Sinking is just another word for neatening. Serrin have mopped seaside villages spotless of life, have shined sailors' lungs with salt water like apples on a shirt hem. See a Serrin toss its hair like dust, rising. See it slip into a drowned sail like a party dress. See it fold the undertow into tight pleats to set carefully aside.

SPOTTED LEPIDOME

Imagine a moth with pale, powdered wings. No, that's not quite right. Here: imagine a bicycle. Now adjust your image of the moth to match the size of the bicycle. That's closer.

Spotted Lepidome do not have a larval state but, rather, begin life fully grown. Not unlike a chrysalis, the Lepidome egg is outfitted with a brassy zipper, which grins open in the act of hatching.

Larkspur and Ghost Pipe's first date was over a hatching Lepidome. The magic of each great wing emerging from almost-death—it was romantic. After the Lepidome flapped away, the editors went home together under the auspices of filing this report. They did not file this report. Thus, Phlox's illustration was drawn with less than complete information. The beast does not actually have wheels—that was a misinterpretation of wording on Phlox's part. It's okay. He did his best with what he had.

The Spotted Lepidome is named for an array of magenta eyes dotting its wings. The marks range between two inches and one foot in diameter. On a typical moth, similar eyelike markings serve to confuse predators into believing they are being watched. In the case of the Spotted Lepidome, however, these marks can actually see. Though it has not been confirmed, we theorize that Lepidome eye spots can see seventeen colors beyond those perceived by the human eye. They may also be able to see the future, sound waves, and the dead.

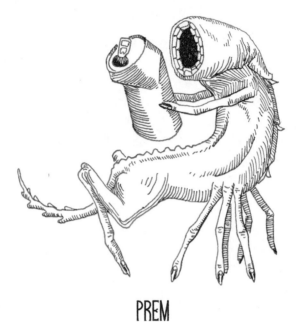

PREM

Anyone will tell you—Prems are a real nuisance. They turned that brand-new pair of shears to rust overnight. They drank the shine from the watering can, crumbling it in five minutes flat. Same with the steering column of Ghost Pipe's car, which fell straight through his Volvo's floor last summer while he was making out with Larkspur in the back seat. Prems have a thirst for good metal. They suck the glint out of it, leaving behind oxidation to drip in red flakes. A Prem's mouth is round and opalescent, like a moon with a hole in it. The best way to keep them out of the house is to leave scrap metal in a pile in the yard. That will satiate them enough to leave the jewelry boxes alone.

YSLANI

When a fruit-bearing tree is planted on a grave, a litter of Yslani will grow during the following drought season. In their fetal stages they resemble plums or dark peaches swelling on the bough. When they grow heavy enough, they drop into the underbrush and uncurl. It will take five days for their eyesight to develop, and until then, the Yslani will blindly claw at the soil in search of water. If one digs deep enough to uncover a body, that Yslani will be shunned from the pack. It will sit alone at the foot of the tree, begging for water in a voice that sounds all too much like the voice of the person buried beneath it. Do not give this Yslani water. We repeat: *do not* give this Yslani water. Walk away. Pretend you do not hear.

DELILINIA

The Delilinia is best known for its musk—a sweet perfume akin to rosewater met with honey and smoke. Serpentine with a golden headdress, it makes a home in blackberry thickets, building its nest in the briar. Poachers hunt it with long iron hooks so they may bottle and stopper the scented oil tucked in the hollow behind its eyes. For those foolish enough to purchase a vial of Delilinia oil in a back-alley medicine show, ennui is inevitable. Merely a dab upon the wrists will drive the wearers to abandon their sweethearts and children. They will lock themselves in attics and do nothing but carve strange glyphs into the walls, and refuse all food save for sweetcakes and elderwine. When the perfume is spent, they will scramble for years along esplanades of foreign cities in search of a peddler carrying the perfume. They will never find one.

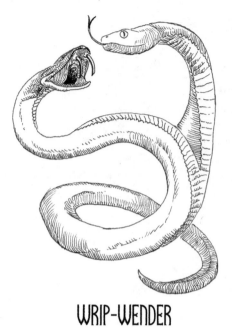

WRIP-WENDER

The Wrip-Wender is a two-headed snake, each side wet-toothed with fatal venom. When the Wrip-Wender reaches mating age, one head will fall in love with the other. It will spend a fortnight writhing against the earth as that head thrashes toward its twin. Eventually, they will meet. Fang will meet throat. Desire will meet body. One head will poison the other. Both sides will die.

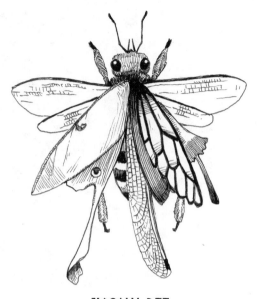

JIGSAW-BEE

No, it is not a chrysanthemum. Those are not petals. It may be beautiful, but the Jigsaw-Bee is more predator than flower. It was not born with so many wings. The Jigsaw-Bee rends wings loose from moths, beetles, dragonflies, and wasps. It gnaws wings off the backs of small bats and fledgling birds still curled in the nest. Then the Jigsaw-Bee affixes this bounty to its own thorax, so it blossoms with dozens of wings from dozens of creatures. It truly is the loveliest little insect, especially when the wings all flit in unison, as if reaching out toward some forgotten home.

OLNIS

The Olnis carries its liver in an embroidered handbag. An evolutionary marvel, this handbag allows the Olnis to process toxins externally, pre-filtering its food outside the body before consumption. It can chew the pulp from nightshade stalks and gulp barrels of bourbon without swooning. Hemlock is a favorite aperitif. When the liver grows too sick, an Olnis will simply snatch a healthy one from another of its kind as a replacement. Olni are constantly sneaking up on one another, snatching handbags, and running off.

The Olnis is an acute judge of character. When taking on a new mate, the Olnis will dip its sweetheart into the handbag. If the sweetheart blisters, the Olnis will promptly dispose of this mate and seek out another. If the potential mate dips clean and quiet into the handbag, like a candlewick into a jar of wax, then the Olnis will embroider a portrait of the sweetheart onto the handbag. Some Olni have dozens of portraits embroidered onto their handbags and some have none.

If Larkspur had had an Olnis handbag, would things have gone better? Probably not.

MOCKING-LOO

Mocking-Loos are almost indistinguishable from rivers. They lure thirsty bucks and wildcats to drink from them. Once ingested, Mocking-Loos lay eggs in the animals' bellies. Three months later, the eggs unlatch in a violent flood, fledglings ribboning out from the hosts' bodies in eager tributaries. There is a simple test to tell the difference between a river and a Mocking-Loo: toss a small handful of cake flour into the water. If it froths up like spittle gone rabid, it is a Mocking-Loo hiding in plain sight.

PANX

Everyone remembers the schoolyard game: Count a Panx's teeth by hand, pressing a fingertip to one, then the next, then the next. While counting, recite the alphabet. When your finger pricks with blood, the letter last spoken will begin the name of the next person you'll love. The game ends by letting the Panx lap the blood off. Return to counting. The number of licks it takes to clean your finger is the number of years before your darling stops loving you. If after a hundred licks the Panx has to be dragged away snarling, unfinished, then you know how lucky you'll be.

Ghost Pipe would like to formally note that he disagrees with the above. He claims that the Panx's reputation is only hearsay, and that is why it stopped licking Larkspur's cut so quickly.

Phlox formally insists that we must focus only on the data, and the data is irrefutably in favor of the Panx's legitimacy.

Ghost Pipe would now like to add (formally) that Phlox is not being very helpful.

Larkspur only weeps and weeps and weeps.

SQUIRM

When Ghost Pipe admitted to Larkspur that he was sorry, but he'd never really loved her, she was so upset that she accidentally manifested a Squirm. At first it wasn't a problem—rather, it was something of a comfort, sleeping on her pillow and accompanying her on errands. But when the weekend ended and research resumed, the Squirm was still there. It followed her to all her lectures. Whenever she had to work with Ghost Pipe out in the field, the Squirm would start to wail. It was a shrill keening, like a saw biting through metal, so loud that everyone in a fifty-foot radius had to cover their ears. It grew worse and worse. It scared off the other beasts. Whenever Larkspur thought about Ghost Pipe or found an old note from him scrawled in the margins of their files or one of his T-shirts under her bed, the Squirm would start yelling again. She tried driving out into the country and abandoning it in the woods, but it found its way back. She tried burying it in the backyard, but it dug its way out. She tried cornering Ghost Pipe in his flower shop and seducing him, and that worked for about two days before the Squirm started up again, louder than ever.

LYLIT

Born to the cranberry bog, burgundy with nectar and new flesh, the Lylit skims below the surface. It feeds on crickets, tadpoles not yet legged, seventeen-year cicadas. It has a certain limber charm, the way it sways in the marsh water like Spanish moss waltzing against wind. Its fins are dainty as Chantilly lace, or red smoke pluming. They are almost too delicate for life, snaring the way a stocking snares, caught in twigs or in a crane's beak. Fishermen comb the Lylits up to take home to their wives, who will don them as fine shawls on Sunday mornings. Yet even draped over women's shoulders, their breath continues in a quiet hush, hush, hush.

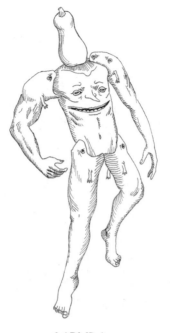

GORLING

Gorlings, unlike most other animals, have five sexes within the species. One of these sexes resembles a man's torso. One resembles a left leg, and one a right. Another resembles a right arm, and another a left. Gorlings will grapple desperately among themselves for five compatible parts in hopes of assembling a complete "coalescence." Once they do, the group is free to walk upright and engage with the world as a human might. As there is no Gorling head, the coalescence has to search out a replacement (a basketball or balloon or boulder or finely packed snowball) if they want to integrate into society. They're obviously fooling no one, but if you see a Gorling trying to fit in, it doesn't hurt to be polite.

RAUST

Rausts resemble jackals with an eagle's beak and wings. They are always born in sets of identical twins. By identical, that is to say each sibling exactly, minutely, matches the other. A tuft of white fur on one's paw appears on the other. A crooked tooth. A bent ear. When one breaks a bone or gets a cut, the injury appears on both bodies. When one feeds, the other is fed. When one falls ill, the other becomes bedridden. However, they differ wildly in mind. When one finds a mate, the other will pace back and forth for days at a time, growling, refusing all amorous advances. When one goes mad, the sane brother will drag the sick brother into the woods and they will stay there among the locust trees until both are well. When one has a secret, the other will have no way of knowing.

In the field, Larkspur noted the admirable loyalty of

Rausts—how even during moments of extreme uncertainty, a Raust will never fully abandon its twin. She pointedly directed this observation at Ghost Pipe, who wilted visibly. Phlox abstained from comment. We three returned to our work, as quietly as possible. The Rausts bowed, in unison, and turned away.

TOMEN

Spidered on eight legs, each shin long as a wheat stalk, the Tomen is more cauldron than not. Its body is an open basin. It fills with storm water, with errant rodents lured to drowning, with sparrow bones and fallen leaves from the sugar maple. Dip a ladle into the tub and sip—bitter as grapefruit left unripe in the root cellar, but it will cure a fever in a pinch. Tomens are ever scuttling through backyards, positioning their bodies beneath fledgling-fat nests and clumsy roofers, hoping a snack might fall from the sky.

CARCORONE

Is it dead? No, though we see why one might believe that. Its skull, devoid of skin, veins, and muscle does imply lifelessness. Its squat torso balances haphazardly on two chicken legs, talons digging into the earth. But despite its aesthetics, the Carcorone is quite lively. Play it a fiddle tune, and it can dance for a full forty days without tiring. Better still, roll down the truck windows and turn the pop radio station up while driving through a square full of Carcorones. They'll all start shimmying, shaking their bare skulls, tumbling over each other in frantic slapstick.

Larkspur brought Ghost Pipe a bouquet of Carcorones, wriggling in a wicker basket. She kept having to push them back down with her metal water bottle so they wouldn't shimmy out. Ghost Pipe said thank you for the gift but it was clear he didn't mean it. Larkspur had been leaving bouquets on Ghost Pipe's doorstep for days (both animal and botanical). *You have to stop this,* Phlox said. But she didn't want to stop loving Ghost Pipe.

Ghost Pipe was beautiful and kind and once, months ago, they lay together in the dark coming up with funny ideas for vanity license plates.

Once you give someone a bouquet, you can't take it back again.

SPARK PANTHER

The Spark Panther can outrun its own soul—faster than the human eye, faster than sound, faster than its sorry prey. Its ghost, not so quick, topples out of its body into the dust. Soulless, the Spark Panther is a vicious hunter. It will rend the larynx from an antelope without remorse. It will gather enough meat to last several months, and then it will feast. Meanwhile, its soul begins the journey back to its host. If the soul arrives too quickly, before the Panther has had time to feed, the creature will be so overcome with guilt at the sight of its slaughtered prey that it will be unable to eat. It will paw at the mournful earth, burying the bodies, its belly empty.

HASTLIT

A delicate crimson bird with translucent wings, the Hastlit is known as a divinatory omen. It is rumored that one can foresee fate by the precise timing or location of a Hastlit encounter. This superstition is immortalized in a well-known nursery rhyme, the first record of which dates back to the seventeenth century. It has since become popular as a football pep cheer, wedding toast, and automated email response:

> *One on the roof for promise;*
> *One on the bough for strife;*
> *One loose in the kitchen or corridor*
> *Will usher the end of life.*
>
> *One in the morn for famine;*
> *One in the eve for mist;*
> *One in a floristry catalog*
> *And someone will be missed.*

MAGLIT

Maglits, after years of urban domestication, are easily taken in as pets. They do a fine job with the dishes, licking china cups clean with their pronged tongues to stack in neat rows on parlor shelves. As carnivores at the highest point on the food chain, it is essential to keep them well-fed. Rarely, a Maglit-owning family will go missing. Rare enough that no one bothers to put it in the paper. Maglits are more asset than harm, after all. How would the laundry get folded without them? How would the floors be mopped so bright and sharp? Best not to meddle. Best to keep quiet about Ghost Pipe's sudden absence, and the deafening hollowness that befell his house on the night that he vanished.

MIRIAPOD

Miriapods are easy to spot but impossible to catch. Often mistaken for streetlamps or car headlights by careless night watchmen, the Miriapod can be identified by the lantern in the center of its forehead. The rest of its body is blank, like the black gap left when a tooth abandons the gum. Miriapods are drawn to empty rooms. Groups gather in warehouses and junkyards. They cluster in the school gymnasium in the middle of the night, when the students are home, asleep. They congregate in empty churches and cemeteries. You'll know they're there because from across town, an abandoned building will ebb light, glow bubbling up through windows and timber slats. But come within a fifty-foot radius, and all will go dark, as if they were never there at all.

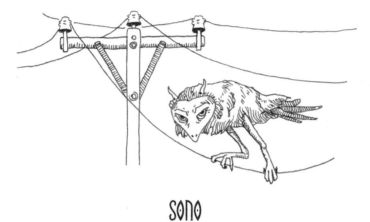

SONO

Sonos perch on the telephone lines and listen through their feet. As the town's whisperings racket from wire to wire, house to house, Sonos grow plump. They are gluttonous eavesdroppers. Before telephones, they stalked telegraph operators and postmen. Before that, they crouched on poets' shoulders and clustered around broadsides nailed to pub walls. They have always heard us. Sonos like bad news best. Not out of cruelty—there is simply a fattiness to the moment when a person realizes the worst is here. When Phlox called Larkspur with news that Ghost Pipe was missing—no note, no text, simply gone—it was such a moment. A buttery quality, muffled as if dipped in batter.

WAXLING

There are freshwater Waxlings and saltwater Waxlings and holy-water Waxlings and hot-water Waxlings. Physically, they are largely indistinguishable from one another—though freshwater Waxlings have an extra row of teeth behind the bottom set, and hot-water Waxlings are slicked in a protective coat of mucus. Otherwise, they share the same brassy scales, stub snout, and webbed hands. While finding a holy-water Waxling in a sacramental font is considered to heighten the potency of baptism, hot-water Waxlings are little more than household pests. Homeowners must be attentive in keeping all boiling pots lidded and drawn baths well monitored, lest a Waxling take up unwelcome residence in a lavender soak or butternut squash soup.

APPLE-GONE

You've seen the Apple-Gone before. Maybe you can't quite place where or when. Maybe your memory slips off the edge of it, the way a mirror spits back light. It was before the cornfield, before Phlox learned to whittle spoons, before the King Poppy Floral Convention and before Ghost Pipe went missing and before the visit to the archipelago where Larkspur lost her favorite sundress. But the Apple-Gone remembers all of us, even if we don't remember the Apple-Gone. It has a memory like a Swiss bank. It remembers many sorts of things—even events it wasn't there to witness. If the Apple-Gone had a mouth, it would be able to tell you all about the Kennedy assassination, and your ex-boyfriend's ATM code, and what the world sounded like before language was born. But the Apple-Gone is mouthless, so none of us will ever know.

LILYMUTT

Born in amethyst caves, Lilymutts spend the first six months of life chiseling armor from stone. Then they press the druzies to their flesh until the amethyst becomes a sort of exoskeleton. Only then do Lilymutts emerge into day. Sun rings off crystal. It is a violent shine, so riotous that a glance will render a viewer immobile for two to three minutes. Lilymutts know better than to look at one of their own kind. However, mistakes can happen. If two Lilymutts gaze at each other, the glare ricochets back and forth indefinitely, imprisoning them both in permanent paralysis: two violet statues shackled with light.

ARCHILOT

Fear the Archilot: the house with knees. Fear its gait. Fear the insatiable lure toward restlessness. The house has made a gift of wanderlust. See it beside the railroad, all golden and sunslick, tasting of saffron. The Archilot sings whaling ballads by memory, sleeps upon hillsides like a stone, calls women like Larkspur Voyager to groom them for roaming. It plays fetch with hubcaps spat from its own door. Rain stitches through shingle gaps, sneaks in like a thief.

I'm going, Larkspur said, *to find him.*

Phlox frowned. *What makes you think he wants to be found?*
They took him.
Who?
The beasts.

Phlox puts a hand on her shoulder. *Sometimes people just leave.*

Oh, how the Archilot trembles when wet. How it gallops like a whipped mare. All it wants is to charge off the end of this earth.

VELNIP

Larkspur left town and began to search, employing a Velnip as her guide. Velnips' tracking skills are unparalleled, and they navigate more precisely than a GPS. If he was out there, alive or not, the Velnip would find him.

The Velnip is a six-legged beast with a tail like a lion's, born in the marble quarries. They cannot heal naturally, so to cover an open sore, they fashion patches from other animals' hides and stitch the patches on using a long thorn. When game is scarce, Velnips have been known to tear swaths of their own flesh free in order to cover the wounds of their mates or young. Larkspur can relate. We all feel beholden to those we love, even when they can give us nothing in return.

KEEL

Keels are useless at running, being so stubby-legged, and tend to trip over their own droopy ears. They are an easy catch for a wolf or fox. Having no practical means of escape, the Keel has developed another method to avoid being devoured: at night, a Keel will track down a pack of predators and nuzzle against the mass. It will whisper compliments into their ears as they sleep (*Oh, pretty monster, I love you the way the moon loves blinking, you are more beautiful than a violin, you are the only poppy in the garden, we are married and I am hanging clean white linens on the line, my strawberry, my creek bed*). As it mutters, it rubs its small flanks against the danger. It slips away before sunrise, cloaked in the enemies' scent. When the predators awaken, they are lazy and sweet and no matter what they do, they cannot muster the sharpness to hunt.

ALBIT

They come when the snow comes, but leave no footprints. No shadow will settle on them. They are wan as buttermilk, narrow as a flagpole, as if the whole body is a pale arm, reaching. Note how they crane over ice banks, their eyes large as billiard balls, their breath steaming. In some cultures, far from here, they believe that Albits are the ghosts of villagers taken by fever during winters past. Not living to see spring, they are doomed to lope evermore through snowdrifts, yearning for warmth. The florist community dismisses such farfetched lore. Albits are like any other animal, despite what they, or anyone else, might insist.

YUNE

Yunes were human once. They nursed babies and baked bread and made love beneath the shade of the willow trees. Then they were drowned in the bog on the edge of town. The marshlands kept them flawless. Their skin tanned tight as a drumskin, sealing their spirits inside like caged dogs. Snarling against their enclosure, the ghosts grew frantic, then foolish, then sick. By the time the bodies rose out of the silt, the ghosts had been trapped too long. They had become something new.

There's an urban legend about a Yune that snuck into a high school party. Some kids were playing spin the bottle in the root cellar, and the Yune joined in. First Jackie spun and had to kiss Ryan; then Ryan kissed Dale; then Dale kissed Nadia; then

Nadia kissed the Yune, and when she did, the Yune's ghost slipped through its parted lips and into Nadia's mouth. It slithered down her windpipe and into her lungs, where it made a new home beside Nadia's own ghost. There aren't many girls with two ghosts in one body. She became quite the local celebrity. Talk shows brought her on to hear her bicker with herself in dead languages she had never been taught. Then they would hand her a small porcelain dish, into which she would cough up a mouthful of mud.

SHE-JACKLIS

A little girl with the head of a coyote, the She-Jacklis is a domestic parasite, inhabiting the homes of families who have lost a child. The She-Jacklis is a master of mimicry. It will crawl into the child's empty bed and howl. It will scrawl notes in the missing child's handwriting to slip under every door in the house. It will put on all the child's clothes, so long untouched in the closet, and will study itself in the mirror for hours.

HARROW

A Harrow's face is rarely seen. They are too handsome—vulgar with beauty, so that to gaze upon one feels like reading a letter you were not meant to see. To conceal themselves, the females grow bone masks and the males whittle masks from cherry wood blanched with lemon juice. Harrows remove their masks only once a year, on the first warm rain of spring. It is the night when salamanders scuttle up from the creek and the soil goes black. If a human sneaks up on a Harrow when its face is uncovered and sees its true visage, the Harrow is beholden to them. Anything the human tells it to do, it must obey. *Dance,* the human may say. *Leave your pack,* the human may say. *Love me,* the human may say. *Give me children as beautiful as you. Burn your mask in the woodstove. Stay inside and let no one see you and press my cotton shirts on the ironing board until the steam dizzies you, you pretty, pretty thing.*

[   ]

There's nothing to say about [   ]. No one has done any research on [   ]. Every time a florist has attempted to study a [   ], they have forgotten what they were doing within half an hour and returned to the lab empty-handed and confused. Whenever anyone starts thinking about [   ], they quickly think of something else instead. Plenty of people have seen a [   ] (they must have, aren't [   ] everywhere?), but no one can remember what they look like. All that is known for sure is that they tend to frequent tow lots, and are often seen near orbs of light hovering just above the

Editors' note: We can't recall what creature we were writing about, so find ourselves unable to complete this page. Please disregard this entry. Do not speak of it. Do not ask us about it. Please tear it from your copy of the text.

SLIVORING

Newborn Slivoring babies, tiny as pinto beans, crawl down the throats of empty beer bottles. Within the glass, the Slivorings will grow just large enough that they cannot slip back out. The bottles protect them from the elements and meddling hands— though on too hot a day Slivorings will grow agitated and begin to hum in harmony. After the thermostat hits eighty-five degrees, bar dumpsters across town sound like someone tried to recycle a barbershop quartet. In the summer of '98, Slivorings sang for a record-breaking sixty-two days without rest. The noise was so obtrusive that the city was evacuated. When a group of unknowing travelers passed through, they found a ghost town swollen with mysterious music that seemed to come from nowhere and everywhere all at once.

CAIRTH-TONGUE

The man has been running for days, and the Cairth-Tongue has been chasing him. By "running," that is to say he has been driving a 1967 Ford F-100 pickup truck. The Cairth-Tongue is chasing him on foot. It will catch up soon. It gallops on two horses' legs, two spiders' legs, two tigers' legs, and two legs of steel. It has a woman's flanks. Coiled behind its teeth is a six-foot whip. The man may have held up a convenience store, or he may have murdered his brother, or set the stables aflame. He may simply have tired of fieldwork and bouquets, and decided to take a long drive, and may be a bit of a coward on top of that. The Cairth-Tongue has a particular taste for cowards. And when the Cairth-Tongue decides to chase, it chases.

MOORY ROOT

Moory Roots embed themselves in vegetable patches and wait to be dug up with the harvest. Knobby with rouged joints, one can easily be mistaken for a yam or a rutabaga. When chopped up for stew, the Moory Root does not die. On the contrary, each individual fragment grows into a new, fully formed Moory Root. Those new Moory Roots will take up a blade and begin to dice one another, and the process of multiple fission reproduction continues. Soon the kitchen overflows with Moory Roots. Moory Roots spill out open windows and fill cabinets. They roll into every bedroom of the house until they reach the ceiling and start popping one by one from the chimney. Once the owners of the house have fled, the Moory Roots will host a big family party. Guests will run around lopping bits off one another, and new guests will pop up from the fallen pieces. Moory clans throw the best parties in town.

WILK

Larkspur has fainted. There was not enough air in the room; a Wilk came and sucked it all out. Larkspur made a mistake, calling the Wilk there. She hoped it would make her feel good. The search for Ghost Pipe had been going nowhere, and it had been too long since Larkspur had felt anything good at all, so she filled a small china dish with mugwort and yarrow root and corn husks and then lit a beeswax candle and held the flame to the dish so the contents fizzled and spat, and she called out the Wilk's call (which we cannot repeat here because we mustn't summon the Wilk), and the Wilk, as it always punctu- ally does, appeared. Then it breathed in deep until all the air was gone, and Larkspur passed out.

When she woke up, she asked the Wilk what had happened.

You had a great time, said the Wilk. *A real doozy of a time. Hell, best time you've had in months.*

But I don't remember anything, she said.

Well, ain't that just the way, said the Wilk. Then the Wilk punched Larkspur in the shoulder, like old pals will do, except harder, before disappearing.

BASTULON

First, they believed their hair was a blessing.

Furless and too skeletal to survive winter, the Bastulons begged the old spirits for warmth. When they grew mute from pleading and their hands had warped from clasping too tightly against the cold, they noticed the first strands prickle up from their scalps. Soon, crimson locks galloped in ringlets all the way down to their ankles. It never tangled nor dirtied. It refracted light, shining like lava against the snow. The Bastulons wove it around themselves and were grateful.

In spring, photographers came. Then young men with spidery hands. Then poachers. Everyone wanted to touch the hair, or braid it into elaborate ropes, or cut it off to sell to shampoo companies. The poachers didn't care if the Bastulons survived the hunt, as long as they came away with hair to sell. The spider-handed men didn't care if the Bastulons ran from them, as long as they ran slow enough to be caught and stroked.

The photographers didn't care about the Bastulons at all—only the brilliant shade of scarlet bulleting by their lenses as the Bastulons fled. After a year, the torment became too much to carry. On the first freezing night of winter, the Bastulons passed a pair of dressmakers' shears between them. They abandoned their curls by the roadside. Then, hand in hand, they walked naked toward the frost.

BLUE-BELLIED IB

Ever since Ibs figured out how to use the phone, it's been prank calls day and night. They're terrible jokesters because Blue-Bellied Ibs cannot lie. Instead, they'll ring you to tell it to you straight:

> *The recycling is all going to the landfill. If you'd kept practicing the fiddle, you'd be good by now instead of dreadful. That comb-over isn't fooling anyone. One day, you too will die.*

> *Remember how you lay together, in the back of the flower shop, the air drowned in gardenia? He'll never hold you again.*

> *You could have loved her—you simply chose not to.*

They're purebred soothsayers. It's okay to hate that. It's okay to shoot the messenger. Rotisserie Ib is a good, filling meal, and if you eat it, you won't have to listen to the truth anymore, ever again. Easy.

SEED VULPES

Most foxes are birthed hot and mammalian. The Seed Vulpes is not most foxes. It is born from a splitting pomegranate. Once free of this womb, it carries the fruit beneath its tongue—little blood drops sweet to the taste. It has been known to leave single seeds on the closed eyes of women abandoned by lovers. When the women wake, they find the Seed Vulpes at the foot of the bed, whistling. It whistles all the tunes the women's lovers once hummed over the kitchen stove and recites their favorite comical vanity plates. When the women reach out to pet the Seed Vulpes, it grins, and the women decide it is better left untouched.

If a woman chooses to eat the pomegranate seeds left upon her eyes (as Larkspur may or may not have done), it can serve as an antidote to the sorrow the lover left behind. The seeds will take root inside the woman. They will sprout and tangle, will grow and grow and will not stop growing. Branches will extend into her fingertips and her knees, bloom into her throat, filling the emptiness her beloved's abandonment gouged out. No more hollows. No more need. Only a sapling, thorny with claws, widening by the day.

NAWL

At the crest of its wet, dark tentacles is a torso. At the peak of its torso is its head. Supporting its head is its throat. In the middle of the throat is a switch.

Switch it on, and the Nawl feels the way anyone feels. Its life, like any life, is a series of small griefs. Sweethearts come and the Nawl flickers awake, its many limbs blooming like lilacs. Sweethearts go and the Nawl writhes in the murk, remembering. Fear comes and the Nawl squeezes shut. Fear goes, and the Nawl unravels. Its heart swells and retreats, swells and retreats, swells and retreats again.

But when the little grievings grow too many, the Nawl flips the switch off. Then it no longer feels anything. It floats silently in black pools filling with stormwater. It watches the sky, unmoved by the waxing and waning of the moon. It wants for nothing.

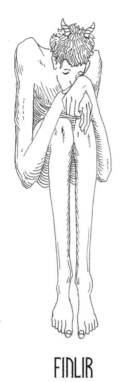

FINLIR

Finlirs are lanky creatures with arms so long they must keep their elbows folded so that their hands do not scrape the ground. Their knees, too, are ever-bent and their shoulders hunched, for Finlirs often feel too unwieldy for this world. They are shy, afraid of taking up space. If you have ever done something you regret, you already know all about them. We have endured a Finlir following us, lapping at our guilt as if it were honey. We know well the laments that shook from our lungs as we remembered our mistakes, and the hum of satisfaction from the Finlir as it drank.

Most people believe that Finlirs feed on the guilt itself. This is not true. They are not as malevolent as they seem. On the contrary, they are nourished by the small acts of forgiveness we grant ourselves in time; each sigh of kindness we accept. Do not begrudge Finlirs their feast. If we do not forgive ourselves for our indiscretions, the Finlirs will die.

Ghost Pipe watched his own Finlir starve—and did nothing.

LOORUS

Some people say the Loorus looks like a man. Others say a hare. Others compare it to a stone or a nickel or a bowl of milk, filling and emptying and filling again. Once, many months ago, Larkspur and Ghost Pipe lay on a picnic blanket and watched the Loorus while sharing a bag of Red Vines. Ghost Pipe buried his face in Larkspur's hair. *You're missing it,* she said, for the Loorus had begun its rare molting of shadows. *I don't care,* he whispered, and in that moment, it was true.

The Loorus hovers above the horizon line, a nocturnal animal nibbling at the fatty dusk. When it grows thirsty, it tugs the tide toward its lips. It is easily insulted, so don't mess with it. Call it by a false name, and the Loorus will make all your exes call you on the same night. Yes, it has that power, and yes, it's that much of a jerk. In the ancient times, scholars worshipped it. They studied it through telescopes. They logged its movement across the sky in little notebooks. They didn't realize it was alive.

Today, Larkspur and Ghost Pipe watch it molt again through separate windows, worlds apart. Are they thinking of each other? That is not for this document to know.

Phlox remains at the office, alone, and finishes the work we started.

ROSE-BEARERS

By the time we concluded our research, two of us were only Rose-Bearers. The lost never truly come back as they were, even when they do. Time can only move forward. There are no organs in a Rose-Bearer. Not anymore. Only petals—red and silken, telltale with their saccharine perfume.

Many florists must be Rose-Bearers by now. Too many of us have confused hunter and hunted. Confused monster with lover. Confused animal with self with a road map of the city limits. Too many of us have been vanished or been swallowed or have fallen asleep in a predator's arms. Too many of us have eaten meat tainted with unspoken things that would remain, forever, unspoken.

When a Rose-Bearer is slit open like an envelope, petals spill onto the floor. The room fills with flowers. Half beauty and half thorn, like everything.

A LILY IS A LILY

IF HE HAD GROWN plump from a year's worth of madeleines and chocolate twists and silky rounds of brie, no one could tell—any new softness had melted from him as soon as he returned home, the stretched taffy of his limbs as sinewy as they had ever been. The boy did, however, maintain a certain *rosiness*, acquired during his schooling overseas—a lightening in the cheeks and lips. Tristan D. Weeber had spent one June to the next studying nineteenth-century French literature at the Sorbonne in Paris. He was ungainly with the language, despite claiming fluency on his application, but an unwearied enthusiasm nudged his professors to err on the side of forgiveness. He had eyes the color of a polished oak floor and beetle-black ringlets of hair, drooping lazily to his earlobes. He dressed well enough, or at least, was proficient in buying clothes that fit, which was more than most of the young men his age could boast. Whether this was his own wisdom or the product of Lily's gentle urging was anyone's guess.

There had been other girls in the past—but none like Lily. Tristan's high school relationships had been brief, trivial affairs. Girls he'd dated out of convenience or boredom or both. One had bought him an expensive fountain pen for his birthday, which he still used, but otherwise, the past girlfriends left little lasting influence. In fact, if asked where he'd gotten the fountain pen, he wouldn't be able to recall.

By the time Lily met him at a bar-basement poetry reading in Paris, he'd nearly concluded his collegiate junior year abroad—and still hadn't fallen into any approximation of love. It's hard to say which drew Lily in more: Tristan's eagerness, or a sort of charming ineptitude in his attempts to recite a poem by Baudelaire in the original French. Tristan, however, knew exactly what of Lily enchanted him: everything.

She had long blonde hair to her hips, bright as spun glass, and a peony-pink glow hovering just below her skin. While everyone else at the microphone that night read a poem, Lily brought a violin to the stage and played a tune so lively and sweet that her hands seemed to shimmer against the instrument's throat. She had been born and raised in southern France, but spoke English with more nuance than Tristan himself, having learned the language from watching American TV shows. The two quickly became companions. Less than three weeks into the romance, Tristan decided that he loved Lily more than he had loved anyone or anything in his life. He promptly told her as much.

But by summer, his visa was up. He was forced to leave Lily and return to Connecticut. It seemed an unfathomable cruelty. When the plane first lifted off the tarmac at Charles de Gaulle, he had been overcome with a terrible sense of *wrongness*. Flying, he decided, was a perfect mirror for heartache: a person is strapped into place with no control of where they're headed, hurling too quickly through time, half nauseated, never quite sure when this awful, trapped feeling would end. Nine hours in flight and two layovers later, Tristan was on one side of the Atlantic and his one true love on the other. The waters seemed to him a colossal torment. How could something so massive even exist? A sprawling beast, poised at his feet with the sole intent of keeping him and Lily apart. Well—he would just have to be even bigger than the ocean.

∽

The looming water tower on the eastern side of his hometown had been out of use for at least thirty years, and built many decades before that. Locals referred to it as Paul Bunyan's Spider. It craned skyward on four steel legs, diagonal cables running between them and a single narrow ladder etching up the side. The basin itself had a rounded belly drooping beneath a squat metal cylinder, which was graffiti-slicked and bloody with rust. A rickety platform with thin railings looped the barrel like Saturn's rings. At one point, there must have been a metal hat perched on top to keep the tank enclosed, but it had long since collapsed inward. Tradition dictated that every graduating high school senior must climb the tower during their final semester and sing the school fight song— but during the summer, the structure sat untouched, sinking into its own creaking body.

Tristan ascended at dusk. He held a flashlight in his teeth, a messenger bag over his left shoulder. The ladder growled under his weight. Wind needled through the pines below and the tower moaned.

Paul Bunyan's Spider was the tallest point in town. From the top, you could see as far as Danbury. Tristan would write Lily's name across the side of the tower, six feet tall and fifteen feet wide, so that his love for her could echo out across all of Connecticut. His love would bounce off shop windows and parked cars, bound down alleyways, reverberate off the asphalt and wiggle along creek beds until it galloped all the way down to the ocean. His bag was heavy with spray paint cans. His hands, tremoring. His heart, a live wire. He lifted the first can, popped off the lid, and raised it to the tower's chest.

That's when the ghost girl spoke.

"Is that for me?"

She was perched on the rim of the tank, her legs dangling over the edge. When Tristan yanked his head up to look, the figure had already vanished into the tub.

"Hello?" he called up toward the open mouth of the tank. "Is someone there?"

A single note unfurled into the air—low and hollow as a sigh. Then more, like fat little moths of sound fluttering up from the tank. Someone inside the tower was playing a violin. It was a song Tristan had heard before.

He hoisted himself back onto the ladder and scrambled toward the top. Music ricocheted off the metal walls, and Tristan crested the edge of the basin, where he peered down into the hollow dark. And there she was. Lily. Lily, here, in Connecticut. Sitting inside a water tower. Waiting for him.

At least, the ghost girl looked every bit like Lily. They were identical: same ruddy glow to her cheeks, same glassy yellow hair, same eyes, lips, crooked bottom tooth, white sneakers with the laces too loose, same blue jeans with the torn right knee . . . But there were small differences, too.

For one, she didn't seem quite solid. When Tristan squinted, he could see through her torso to steel panels on the wall behind her.

Second, he was only able to see her in the black pit at all because her entire body emitted a pale, green light like St. Elmo's fire or a party glow stick.

Third, and most notably, this Lily's hands were white as marble and shone brighter than the rest of her, as if filled with compressed pearls. One hovered over the fiddle bow, the other swept along the strings. But though the fiddle crooned, her hands never quite touched it. Rather, they seemed to float through the instrument like mist.

Tristan was captivated.

He waited until the tune ended to speak. Or rather, the tune decided to allow another voice a turn. If Tristan had tried to talk before, he wouldn't have managed to—for every tiny muscle in his body, every capillary, every small cell sweeping through the blood was swallowed up by the strange steel-fed song of the glimmering girl.

"Lily? How . . . how did you get here?"

The other Lily rested her fiddle in her lap with her white hands. Those hands—they were as ivory as anything Tristan had ever seen. Whiter than photos of Antarctica. Whiter than a cat's clean, sharp tooth. Whiter than the first winter snowfall with its goose-down hush. Whiter than bone. And shimmering, shimmering.

"Well, that's a stupid question! This is where I live." The other Lily combed her hands through her hair, her knuckles sifting apart like smoke before re-forming, clasped, at her stomach.

Wasn't this Lily? His Lily? She didn't live here—she lived in Paris, in a cheap apartment with a slanted floor in the 5th arrondissement. She had never been to the States. Or Connecticut. And she certainly didn't live inside an old water tower.

"You *are* Lily, aren't you?" he asked, hesitant.

"Of course I'm Lily!" she replied. "But there are so very *many* Lilys—perhaps you've mistaken me for another one."

"Yes . . ." Tristan said. "Yes, that must be it. Another Lily . . ."

As everyone knows, when a person is missed enough, a ghost is born. Say, for example, you have a memory of your sweetheart sleeping in a willow tree's shade, and another of her trying on sunglasses at a mall kiosk. When your sweetheart goes away, you'll be inclined to think of her there beneath the willow whenever you pass it. You'll yearn for her when you stumble by the glasses kiosk on your way to work. And you'll long for her with that sort of longing that webs itself through the entire body, as if a silkworm were spinning fabric of longing inside you, bolts and bolts of silken longing, whole sails of it. And when you don't think you can miss her any more, *pop*, a ghost manifests in the spot she once stood. Ghosts appear all over town, in every place the two of you visited. Eventually, when you can't go anywhere without dodging ghosts, you have to walk right through them.

And if your lost person never set foot in the town where you live? Then the ghosts appear at random.

Ghost Lily stuck up her chin. "You were about to do something very sweet for me, Tristan, and I'd really love if you got on with it." She stared pointedly at the spray can, which he'd stuffed into his jacket pocket.

"Oh! I was, yeah. I mean, for the other Lily. My Lily."

"A Lily is a Lily," Lily of the White Hands replied.

Tristan got to work, and Lily of the White Hands looked on. Along the tower's bruised ribs, thin clouds of paint left gleaming snail trails. An *L* tall as a man with turquoise serifs. An *I* like the craning neck of a giraffe. And more—finishing with the *Y*'s curling tail, ebullient as a circus poster clapping against night winds. When it was complete, he and Lily of the White Hands leaned back against the railing to admire his handiwork. He felt a sudden need to hold one of her moon-milk hands, and reached to take one in his own. But his palm passed right through.

∾

The next day, Tristan placed an international call to France. He and Lily talked for an hour and forty-three minutes. He told her about the long journey home. About moving back in with his parents, who had strung up a banner in the kitchen reading WELCOME HOME, BIENVENUE! About his mother's absurd new haircut, which made her head look backward. He read Lily a poem he wrote about her on the flight back. He was going to tell her about the Lily in the water tower—but the conversation spiraled off in drunken honeybee loops, lazy with distance. Their two voices grew nectar thick, little flitting wings of conversation blinking, a long summer sigh. And the other Lily never came up.

～

At dusk Tristan returned to the water tower.

He'd pillaged the suitcases still squatting unpacked on his bedroom floor until he'd found one of Lily's long cotton dresses. Unwashed, it still carried her lilac perfume—a parting gift. Now it dangled from his fist as he rattled up the steel ladder.

"Here," he said, reaching the top. "You can have this if you need something else to put on." He didn't know if ghosts tired of wearing the same thing day after day, or even what ghosts could or couldn't wear, but it seemed right to offer. He gave Lily of the White Hands the dress. It fit her perfectly.

"Tell me about the other Lily," said Lily of the White Hands.

You're the other Lily, thought Tristan. He told her anyway.

"She's perfect. Beautiful. The most beautiful girl in the world."

"Beautiful like me?" asked Lily of the White Hands.

"Yes," said Tristan. "Exactly like you."

"What is her least favorite kind of fruit?" asked Lily of the White Hands.

Tristan didn't know what Lily's least favorite fruit was, she'd never told him. He told Lily of the White Hands that *his* favorite fruit was pomegranate and his least favorite was kiwi. Lily of the White Hands was in full agreement.

"I'm sure the other Lily thinks so, too," Tristan said.

Lily of the White Hands had dozens of questions about the far-away Lily. And Tristan loved answering them. He loved nothing more than talking about Lily. When he didn't know the answers, he asked Lily of the White Hands what her preference was. He assumed that Lily probably felt the same way. *They must have more in common than just their looks,* thought Tristan. *They must be the same in all sorts of ways.*

❧

Tristan spent more and more evenings in the water tower. While his own Lily breathed and pulsed and ran errands and played the fiddle far on the other side of the Atlantic, Tristan could visit Lily of the White Hands and the distance wouldn't seem so terrible. Plus, Lily of the White Hands had all sorts of romantic ideas for how he could show his love for Lily.

"Maybe I'll write her a letter every day, from now until I see her again," Tristan proposed.

"No, it isn't . . . *sacrificial* enough," said Lily of the White Hands. "You have to prove how you *suffer* for her."

Lily of the White Hands' most inspired suggestion was to collect five hundred four-leaf clovers and mail the lot to Paris. *Now that's a labor!* Tristan thought when offered the idea. He stole an empty cigar box from his father's study to house the treasures in. He would have to search every day for the entire summer—possibly longer. There were tricks he would have to learn, patterns and shapes he would train himself to spot to make the task easier. But not too much easier. This was intended to be toil, after all. A tedium. Lily would open the box and know precisely how vibrant his dedication to her was. These would be no ordinary good luck charms—this was love.

And so by day, Tristan combed his neighbors' lawns for shamrocks, while by night, he clattered up the ribs of Paul Bunyan's Spider. Lily of the White Hands would play her violin, or listen as Tristan read to her, or simply run her vaporous hands through Tristan's hair. Her touch: a breeze, passing.

～

Summer crawled on, and Tristan's health began to fizzle. He wasn't sleeping. Every witching hour was spent with Lily of the White Hands. Dark lakes had flooded beneath his eyes, and his movement resembled a spooked animal. The more time he spent with her, the more he longed for Lily. He had lost count of how many times he'd reached for Lily of the White Hands without thinking, only to stumble forward, through her. Each failed moment of contact slid another coal into his belly to smolder. His knees were raw from kneeling in gravel, searching for clovers. His heart was a screen door swinging on shrieking hinges. But how could he give up his night visits? To be near a Lily, any Lily, was better than no Lily at all. And this Lily was so *nearly* a full Lily, so *nearly* his.

"Do you ever leave this tower?" asked Tristan one evening, while Lily of the White Hands hovered her head over his lap, her yellow hair spread across his knee like fine sand. Every so often, she'd forget to hold herself rigid, and the back of her head would sink into his leg. Tristan shifted his weight beneath Lily of the White Hands' weightlessness. "I just mean . . . I was wondering . . . well. I was wondering if we might hang out other times, instead. In other places. Not just Paul Bunyan's

Spider. You'd like my parents' house, I think, and you could sleep in a real bed. I could see you in the light."

Lily of the White Hands considered the request. "Yes," she said, "I suppose that would be all right."

$$\backsim$$

Lily of the White Hands began accompanying Tristan as he searched for clovers. She would often find them first, but Tristan insisted she never tell him, lest his romantic labor become any less genuine. When he got a summer job pumping gasoline at Stan's Gas Mart down the road, she would appear there, too. She flickered oddly in daylight, slipping in and out of sight. Sometimes she was as visible as a normal, living person, and other times she was little more than a sun glare on a car windshield. She would shrink and grow. When Tristan missed Lily the most, Lily of the White Hands would elongate until she was taller than a house. In moments when the pain of Lily's absence lessened, Lily of the White Hands shrunk so small that Tristan could carry her in his pocket.

She came to live in Tristan's bedroom and quickly took to sleeping in Tristan's bed, beside him. The boy's parents were amenable to the houseguest. They may have found her incorporeal form a bit odd, but they weren't judgmental people. Sometimes in the night, Tristan became so overcome with longing for Lily that he would bring his lips to her misty fingertips and inhale, as if he could draw her into his lungs.

Lily of the White Hands had taken to wearing Lily's old dress exclusively. She consumed no food, nor drink, at least none Tristan could see. She didn't seem susceptible to weather, though when a heat wave struck, the pair began going to the movies to escape the skillet. Their taste in films was impeccably matched. They loved and they hated in tandem.

Lily of the White Hands was the perfect girlfriend. Tristan couldn't touch her, so he never stopped wanting her. She couldn't leave him because she was already gone. She remained permanently lovely, like a human, but softer somehow, as if her imperfections were sloughed off by the Otherworld. Like any gaseous form, she could expand and contract to fill the container of his heart in whatever way it needed to be filled.

Tristan woke with his hands inky with rust. He dreamt of long spools of gauze unraveling, and soon, he dreamt of nothing at all. He was hungry all the time, but not for food—he craved cotton and chlorine and silt. He craved her yellow hair. Most of all, he longed for her glistening hands to become solid, bodied things. To reach out for him and make wicked contact. The wanting was terrible and wonderful. He read an article in the newspaper about a woman hit by a train, and for days, frothed with envy at the notion of collision.

∽

"Don't think I can't see you getting handsy with that dead girlfriend of yours on shift."

Stan of Stan's Gas Mart leaned against the car wash door, smoking a cigarette.

"She's not dead," spat Tristan, offended.

"Oh yeah? I ain't never seen a living girl who can float through the damn walls like that."

"She's not dead," Tristan insisted again. "She's just . . . not here."

"Well, whatever the hell she is, she's freaking out the customers. Tell her to stay home."

The phone rang from inside the convenience store. Stan mashed his cigarette out with his thumb and trudged inside to answer.

"Hey, kid! It's for you. It's that goddamn girlfriend of yours. Tell her not to call you during work."

Tristan was halfway to the counter before he realized that Lily of the White Hands wouldn't be able to *pick up* a phone. Something must be wrong. Was she *in* the phone lines? Tangled in the electrical snaps and hisses that bulleted between Connecticut's telephone poles? He doubled his pace.

"Hello?" he answered, his throat constricting with panic.

"Tristan?"

The voice on the other line sounded like Lily of the White Hands, but firmer.

"Tristan, it's Lily. I'm here. I'm in Connecticut. I know, I should have given you a heads-up, but I just missed you so much, and I wanted to surprise you, and well, I was going to go to your parents' house but I realized I didn't know the address, so I'm calling you now instead. I'm at the Greyhound station, and maybe it was stupid to come all this way, but I'd really love to see you . . ."

Tristan ran three miles to the bus terminal without stopping for a breath.

∽

From twenty feet away, he spotted her. She was waiting on a wooden bench in front of the station. Yes, the Lily he longed for, his Lily, here and bodied and present!

Though still half blurred with distance, he could already imagine the feel of her, the velvet of her lips, the firm motion of her hands, her hands, which would finally drag across him like twin irons, searing hot. The honey of her mouth. The silk of her skin. The obliterating moment of collision.

But as he grew nearer, something was wrong. Her hair was duller than he remembered—not spilling loose like molten gold, but smothered atop her head in a scrunchie, matted from travel. Her face was dotted with tiny mistakes—pockmarks and sleep lines, her lips chapped, a pimple above her left eyebrow. When she called his name, the volume of her voice startled him. Even her hands were off—her fingernails chewed, cuticles rough around the edges. And when she ran to him and threw her arms around him and kissed him, he was horrified by her vulgar *solidity*. It felt crass, this glow-less, bony girl who tasted nothing like the honey he remembered. Her body was so loud. So easy.

A small, familiar presence now moved in his shirt pocket.

"Wait," he said. "There's someone I want you to meet."

This will fix it, Tristan thought, *if the two of them join, merge back into one, everything will be like it was.*

He plucked Lily of the White Hands from his pocket like a silk kerchief and shook her out. She ballooned into a girl. Lily looked straight through her, as if she couldn't see her at all. And side by side, the contrast was even more grotesque. One Lily—radiant, satiny, her very presence humming with starglow. A familiar shimmer to her, as if her body were made of mirrors. Her feet hovering just above the ground like a held breath. The other girl—racked with human defect, grossly concrete in her hereness. Her mannerisms lousy with gravity. Every detail of her too sharp, too true, too present. She left nothing to long for, to reach toward, and miss.

Tristan fled the bus station. He did not look back.

∽

"I have something for you. A present."

He had brought only a small suitcase to the water tower. He wouldn't need much. A pillow. A few changes of clothes. Enough food to last. And when the food ran out, well, he'd make do.

Grinning, he revealed a small package wrapped in crisp brown paper. Lily of the White Hands couldn't hold it herself, so Tristan opened it for her. He laid the clovers out in rows along the floor, until the bottom of Paul Bunyan's Spider was cloaked in brittle green. Lily of the White Hands counted them aloud. All the way to five hundred. She reached for Tristan. Tristan reached for her. He kept reaching.

DEAR HENRIETTA

I WRITE TO YOU from a friend's attic, long overdue. It's been such an awful while since we caught up. The fault is mine—I've been terrible at keeping in touch with friends these last few years, ever since Peter and I split. It isn't like his abandonment came as a surprise . . . but I was always wildly skilled at fooling myself into looking the other way when it came to Peter. Call it a well-honed talent. I was wearing that blue long-sleeved dress when he left me (the one I wore to your housewarming party in Brooklyn, remember?) and I haven't been able to bear wearing it since. It's a shame. I always loved that dress.

At any rate, I've been shuffling through odd jobs since then, moving in and out of apartments that feel either too small or too large, as if I don't quite know the space I take up anymore. Most recently, my old friend Claire has been generous enough to let me reside in her attic for a month or so. I have a little wooden desk that faces a tight-lipped window, where I now sit. The window is home to a colony of wasps, which I spent the better part of an afternoon gawking at as they constructed a marvelous paper citadel. A few feet away I have a twin bed on a frame that doesn't creak and a small reading lamp teetering on an overturned fruit crate, which serves as a nightstand. The eaves overhead meet at a sharp angle, which despite my best attempts, never fails to remind me of Peter's widow's peak. It seems even architecture has taken to taunting me!

However, what this room reminds me of even more than Peter's receding hairline is your little barn in Switzerland, where I stayed that autumn I visited you—six years ago, was it? Yes, it must have been, because it was nearly seven years ago that you stayed with Peter and me in California for almost a full summer, and I think you extended the invitation in turn as a means of returning the favor. I had just left my teaching job at Antioch, and had spent the summer in Germany before descending into the Opulent Expanse, as you called it, to see you. Peter couldn't get out of work, so I was a lone voyager for the first time since we'd been married. I recall that the very week I arrived was the same week you decided to tell *your* husband that you were leaving him for your American lover, and would be moving to the states the following month. Henrietta, I *understand* a woman must do what feels right, but lord, couldn't you have waited until you didn't have houseguests? I know, I know, it's selfish of me. But remember that dreadful evening when we powered your television with a generator battery and watched that film in German without any English subtitles, which, from what little I could tell, was about incest at a dinner party? And do you recall how whenever one of you left the room to use the outhouse, the other would turn to me and say truly despicable things about the other (yes, he was doing so as well, it wasn't only you—and no I won't tell you what he said, even if I *could* remember). It wouldn't all have been so bad in a normal house—but no running water, no electricity, no *telephone*, for god's sake, with which to contact the outside world and avoid your domestic nonsense. And all this surrounded by one hundred fifty acres of farmland, with not another person around for miles.

I'm sorry, I don't mean to gripe. You know I adored the time I spent with you, picking black currants for jam, wandering through the forest, learning to embroider tiny red and blue *x*'s into white linen. And anyway, I don't bring up that visit to complain about your squabbles with Luca. What I mean to address is that room in the barn attic, so very like the room where I sit now. Being here, it's made me feel the time has come to tell you something . . . singular . . . that I experienced during my stay in Switzerland. It's something I never mentioned to you at the time. I don't know *why* I never mentioned it. Perhaps I thought I was imagining things, touched by the isolation and the imposing wilderness. But, Henrietta, here in my sweet hideaway in Claire's attic, so very much the twin to that room on your old farm—it made me think of this dream, or happening, or whatever it was. This *incident* that I, for whatever reason, kept from you.

～

The room was at the top of a storage barn, yes? I recall the bottom half of the building was full of tools for hitching the horse to plow, as well as the various pieces of junk your husband had collected and refused to relinquish (dozens of tin cans, broken wheelbarrows, a corduroy armchair with a hole chewed straight through the back where some animal had built a burrow). I also remember that your husband told me not to let the cat inside, because he hated the cat and didn't want it setting foot in any building he owned. You, of course, whispered, *We'll sneak the cat in. She'll sleep on your bed!* as soon as Luca was out of earshot.

The room itself was scant, not unlike this one. No dresser or closet or locking door, but it did have a bed mounded with quilts you had hand-stitched yourself and a single feather pillow. Next to the bed was a small oak table supporting two tapered candlesticks in a brass candelabrum and a couple of books. I can even tell you which books they were, because I have the distinct memory of reading them by headlamp each night after I had climbed the stairs to bed. One was an illustrated edition of Swedish fairy tales. The other, Rilke's *Letters to a Young Poet*. Both proved to be perfectly suited to the environs. The final furnishing of the room, by far the most luxurious, was a thick sheepskin rug that pooled across the wood slats of the floor like spilled cream.

I must have missed Peter desperately, then, because once in bed, wrapped in hand-knit blankets, I would play a little game with myself—a test, really. I would try to imagine his scent, to conjure it up so fully that I might bring it into the room. First, I would break it down into ingredients. The cotton and detergent of his nightshirt.

Sweat against his skin. Deodorant. His hair, a day shy of washing. And then those inexplicable perfumes a person generates—in Peter's case, grapefruit and hazelnut, which always seemed to waft behind him like an olfactory shadow. I would lie there, the candle huffed out, my open eyes unseeing in the dark, and mapping layer by layer, I would try my best to manifest him.

But, just when I could nearly feel the weight of him against me, another musk crept in. A musk that didn't belong to Peter. An interloper. It slinked in not unlike that cat your Luca detested so much, silent and unseen and entirely unwelcome. It was a heady scent, of hay and oil and beastliness. It yanked my reverie toward wildness, a mammalian fragrance, something untamed. First I tried to banish it, but it refused to be driven out. It wrapped itself around my imaginary Peter, sullying him. When it was clear the aroma would not vacate willingly, I instead set to identifying it. At least then I might find its origin and remove it from the room. I fell deeper into my senses. Grass and open air. A bodied heat. Wool. Wool! It was the sheepskin! I leapt up and gathered it from the floor, then marched down the stairwell, depositing the thing in a bin of soldering irons and broken pottery (more of Luca's treasures). Satisfied, I returned to bed, and soon plummeted into sleep.

I dreamt of your pasture. A flock grazed on a jade hillock, Peter alongside—shepherding. I watched them with a wolf's eyes, blood-mad with hunger.

When I woke, the scent of sheepskin had returned to the room so thickly that I choked on my own breath. It lingered like a haunting in the hollow barn, a stain on the clean air. Opening my eyes to the morning, I found myself clutching it. Henrietta, I must have sleepwalked down into the barn and collected the fleece from the rubble . . .

∽

Do you remember how we walked to the library that following day? It was a three-mile walk from your house, and we kept crossing back and forth over the tarmac to stay on the safer side of traffic. Of course, there was no traffic, but you wanted to take every precaution. When we finally arrived, you found a book of Victorian funeral portraits and xeroxed page after page to take home. For the fashion, you said. You liked the corpses' evening coats.

I was only half with you that day. I think you could tell. I recall you saying something about how Luca must have made the coffee too weak that morning, and that Luca made the coffee too weak every morning, and maybe it was because Luca was too weak a man himself. Henrietta, I'll tell you now, it wasn't for lack of strong coffee. During the whole walk to the library, and the time we spent wandering the stacks, and the journey home—a good four hours, in total—the scent of the sheepskin clung to me. That same sullied perfume of lanolin and rain and wool moldering on a dirt floor. Even there, miles from the barn, the scent followed me like a dog. It nipped at my heels. When I held my breath, I could taste it in the back of my throat. So muddy was the air with this smell that I was afraid I would suffocate. Honestly, Henrietta— some part of me truly feared that the sheepskin's aroma would replace my last remnants of precious oxygen and

I'd slip into unconsciousness, never to see my home country again.

I know you're reading this and wondering why I didn't tell you what was happening at the time. I didn't mention it because, even then, I think I knew this wasn't an earthly experience. For one, I was absolutely certain that I was the only one who could perceive the fragrance. I'm not sure why I believed this, but it was something I just *knew*, the way you know instinctively when you're being watched. And second, I had convinced myself of the notion that if I described it all to you, you would ask me to leave your farm and not return.

Have you ever kept a secret for no good reason? Maybe it wasn't juicy enough to tell. Maybe there was no one you liked well enough to tell it to. Or maybe you kept the secret so well, you even kept it from yourself—and when you reached to retrieve it, the secret hovered on the edge of your memory like an insect, batting and batting against a screen door, but fluttering off when you tried to catch it in the cage of your fingers. You know what? I always knew Peter would leave. Even the day before our wedding, I asked him if he was *sure* he was making the right choice. He laughed it off, said I was just suffering from pre-wedding nerves—but I really think I knew. I didn't know why he would leave, or when, but I knew he would.

I'm not sure if you remember this, but when we returned from the library, I said I needed to wash. I claimed it was because I'd sweat so much walking to and from the library, but in truth, it was the odor of the fleece. It made me queasy. You boiled water on the woodstove and filled a washbasin, bucketful by bucketful. I soaked in the living room for over an hour. Finally, lavender soap overtook the stench of wool—if only for a moment.

By dusk, it had returned. I was back in bed, nauseated. It was as if I were smothered in wool, a shepherd pressed in a flock. When I closed my eyes and tried to imagine Peter, I couldn't conjure even the slightest image of him. All I saw were open fields.

I know this is a strange letter. I know that you never asked to hear this story, or hear from me at all, ever again for that matter. But you've made choices, Henrietta, and those choices have consequences.

For hours that second night, I lay awake, trying to ignore the stench. My skin was hot and prickling, itching almost. *Asking* for something. At just past two in the morning, I got out of bed and marched down into the bottom level of the barn, where I'd once again stashed the fleece. As soon as I touched it, the torment hushed. A breeze passed through my body as if I were the pasture, as if I were the meadow where the flock grazed, and the breeze was sweet and cool and steady. I curled up on the sheepskin and immediately, I slept.

The following week, it remained the same. By day, I helped you pack your belongings and kept Luca busy with conversation and company. When you and I were alone, I listened to you talk about your American boyfriend, though you never called him by name. Looking back, I can now see that you were careful to avoid that detail. At the time, I didn't even notice the omission. I was barely there—most of me was in the barn, dreaming of the sheepskin.

Every night, I wrapped myself in it. I slept in later and later. I told you I was ill, remember? I pretended that

Luca's cooking had given me food poisoning, which seemed to satisfy you. You were glad to have more to blame on him. In truth, I was writhing on the barn floor, digging my hands into softened wool.

This part you probably do remember: shortly before I left, Luca found the fleece mutilated in the barn. He assumed the cat had done it. He caught the cat and drowned it in the creek. I didn't stop him or correct him. I didn't open my mouth at all. If I had, he might have seen the hair caught in my teeth, my tongue red and rough.

Are you wondering about the package I've included with this letter? You haven't opened it yet, have you? Don't worry, we'll get to that in time.

Henrietta, do you know what Peter told me when he said he was leaving? He said, "Aren't you glad it isn't with a stranger?" He thought I should be relieved. Ha! Can you imagine? As if leaving me for a friend were some sort of kindness, and our common affection could be something he and I might have in common. Like I hadn't been betrayed at all.

You threw the ruined fleece in the compost pile behind the farmhouse. The next day, when we went out to till the soil, it was gone. "Wolves will always find their prey," you said.

Of course, it wasn't wolves—but you must have known that. I hid the sheepskin in my luggage. When I left, I brought it with me. I returned home to Peter, who though I didn't yet know for sure, was already readying to leave me. You made your plans in tandem. Each little detail. While you were extracting yourself from Luca's bank accounts, Peter was doing the same with ours. But I was too much of a fool to notice—too busy sleeping naked beneath the fleece all afternoon, while Peter was away at work. Each day, I chewed a little corner off, or dragged my nails down its rubbery back. Easier to love an object, no? Wouldn't you say, friend?

I'll admit, I was rather an idiot all these years as to where you two went—Peter left no forwarding address. He just vanished. He always was a coward, our Peter. I spent months searching, but the both of you swept your footsteps clean. And in truth, only half my heart was in the search. The other half, the greater half, was thudding against my pelt, my love, my skin of the lamb.

How did I find you, you're wondering? You may have gone your entire life nevermore hearing from me—if not for Claire. She happened to be attending a wedding in Vermont last month, and who did she spot through the window of a quaint little coffee shop—but her old friend Peter. Henrietta, you may not remember Claire, but you did meet her once, at a cocktail party that summer you stayed with Peter and me. At any rate, she remembered you, well enough to recognize you beside my husband, your hand knotted into his. From there, the small town's directory provided what little more I needed to know.

I recently had a drink with an old colleague, a philosopher who studies time. She told me that time is a filmstrip, already developed. We're like a projector's lens, moving along the strip, able to see only one frame per moment—but the whole reel is already in place. All predetermined. Peter was always headed for you. I was always destined to be alone. But so too, then, was this letter waiting, somewhere on the periphery of time, to find you.

You may open the box now, if you like. Maybe you already have. If you think you can avoid my fate by leaving it closed, I'm sorry to say that isn't how it works. You can already smell the musk rising, can't you? It's yours now. You may have been immune to it before—but no longer. I've been muttering into it for weeks, telling it all about you. Describing your face, your voice, your gentle movements—just as you must have done for me, before I arrived in Switzerland all those years back. How you must have readied the fleece for my arrival. Fed it my name so that when I stepped into that barn, it already knew me, ready to make me fester with obsession so rabidly that I never even saw the wolf prowling at my door. Henrietta, I've been whispering back to it. It's been listening well.

I'll tell you how it will go: First, the dreams. Then, the fever. Soon, you will become so burdened with its presence that you'll neglect your duties. You'll forget my husband. You'll forget your own name. You'll forget to feed yourself, to comb your hair, to open the mail. I know this, because I have lived it. Don't think of it as a curse. Think of it as a promise. We have already lived so many parallel experiences. My beloved in your bed. My footsteps on your farmland. And now—this. A gift. I'm only returning what was always yours.

POSSESSIONS

STEFAN BRINGS THE ROOSTER, bound by the feet and slung over a shoulder. Paula brings the Swiss Army knife, plus a pocketed billiard ball she stole from Rockyside's pool table. I bring the spell book.

The sunflower field reaches up through the gloaming, its gold canopy graying in low light. We wend our way toward center. Bluebells and budding squash form shadows against the soil, elongated by our phones' flashlights. The flower heads nod as we pass, a bobbing auditorium of spectators ushering us through the local farmland known as Sheldon's Plot. After a while, the sunflowers give way to cow corn, too tall for even Stefan to see over. All around, peepers trill their piccolo songs. The rooster, mercifully, is quiet, though Paula is humming "Second Hand News" under her breath, the tempo sped up just enough to stress us out. Overhead, a strawberry moon opens its mouth full and round, as if offering to swallow us up should things not go well tonight. Just in case we need an exit plan.

About half a mile deep into the field, we reach a clearing where the corn yields to a dirt flat. It extends in a ten-foot circle like the eye of a great green hurricane. We drop our stuff and sit down. From the ground, the corn seems endlessly tall, a wall that yearns up and up and up toward the gaping sky. Stefan cradles the rooster like a baby to keep it hushed, rocking it in the crooked elbow of his flannel. Its eyes must be the darkest things I've ever seen—little black gems built of fear and the absence of light. I don't like watching Stefan coddle it like that. It's too sweet. Paula keeps turning the billiard ball over in her hands, passing it back and forth between her palms like a hot coal. Not one of us can stop fidgeting, so I try to put my restlessness to use and open the spell book.

∽

I picked up the book at Goodwill. I think we'd all have felt a little better if I'd found it in an attic among a mess of dried lilac, or had inherited it from a great-great-grandmother, or had it bestowed upon me by a mysterious drifter in a long wool coat—*some* mystical stamp of authenticity. But that's not how it went down. It came right out of the cookbook section of Goodwill, asleep between a volume on candied meats and *30 Meals You Can Make With Mustard!* The spell book itself looked like a novelty cookbook, too, spiral bound with a red plastic coil and fat with photos of women peacocking in seventies hairdos. They clutched quartz crystals and pendulums in their manicured talons. The text was written in a cartoony font in which the first letter of every paragraph twisted into the shape of a witch's hat. The whole thing didn't exactly instill confidence in the author's dedication to the dark arts. But we're desperate. And it's all we have.

~

The book is splayed open on the black ground. Everyone looks up as if expecting me to bugle some declaration or bang a starting gong or give a wedding toast. I could give them what they want, but instead I snap an order.

"Paula—put the ball in the middle."

That's how this will go. No laborious fanfare. No fluff. She does as told. The cue ball glows in the moonlight like the moon's own doppelgänger. I check the book.

"It says to draw a circle around it in the dirt."

Paula takes up a twig and scratches a loop around the ball.

"Okay, now do the same with the chicken."

"Rooster," says Stefan.

"Rooster. Whatever. Make a circle around that, too. Next to the other one."

Stefan dips the rooster onto the soil and tries to drag a circle around it, but the bird keeps squirming. With its feet tied, all it can do is roll, but it's amazing how vivaciously an imprisoned animal can wriggle. Stefan attempts to etch the circle again, but now the thing's squawking.

"Let's do this before someone hears," Paula says.

Stefan pins the rooster down while I trace the circle. The gentleness Stefan had put into cradling the thing is gone. Funny how a person can switch like that. For a moment, I linger on Stefan's sure, strong hands before he catches me looking and I flit back to the page.

"Now someone connect the chicken circle and the pool-ball circle." Lines are dragged into dust. Corn silk floats up from the agitated earth.

"Ready?" I ask. I look to Paula, whose eyes widen.

"Me? I have to do it?"

"I mean, you have the knife," I say.

"Sure, but any of us can use it. Does it have to be me?"

"Stefan, you want to . . . do the honors?"

"Nope."

Paula yanks an ear of corn off a nearby stalk. The plant shivers, the way things do when something that was irrevocably theirs is taken away without warning. A readjustment to lack. A shifting weight. She drags the husk off in three strips, then scrapes an *X* into one of them with the tip of the knife. She clusters the three in her fist so the *X* is concealed, then extends the bundle to Stefan.

"Pick one," she says. He does.

"You too," she says, turning to me. I draw a husk. It's papery and rough like a dried-out cat's tongue. We all look at our husks at the same time. Mine's blank. I say as much.

Stefan shrugs. "Nothin'."

"Shit," Paula says.

"You got this?" I ask her.

"Yeah," she says. She doesn't sound like she means it, but I know she does. We all mean it. None of us wants to be here, but to quote my mom as she quotes the Rolling Stones, *you can't always get what you want.* Paula approaches the rooster, still writhing under Stefan's hand, liquid and shivering, a gray mass of feathered mercury.

"Sorry, buddy," she tells it. She slips open the blade.

∽

The last time any of us saw Aimee—my best friend, Ste-fan's girlfriend, Paula's sister—was at Rockyside. This was nine days ago. We were just over halfway through summer break, the four of us back home in Johnsbury after our first collegiate year (Paula's second). Aimee and Paula were on a sister date. They had decided to become pool sharks, and had agreed to meet for a beer and their first training session at the only bar in town that doesn't card. They were liberal with the rules and the chalk cube, and their cue tips dragged little clouds behind them after powdering. Later, when the police would ask Paula to reconstruct their conversations that night, she would recall it step by step: a hopscotch of one topic to the next. First: the subject of "ferret legging"—a sport that involves trapping a ferret or two in your pants and see-ing how long you can handle them scrambling up and down your pinking thighs. ("It's a real thing! The world record is five and a half hours, held by a coal miner in England—look it up, I swear!") Aimee laughed mid-swig at a description of the tournament hall, causing a fizz of beer to spritz from her nose. This led to reminiscing about the date with Jake Berman where Paula snorted out a clump of white rice, which slipped into talk of other past boyfriends, then to present boyfriends, and ultimately devolved into a one-upmanship contest of sex stories—the final specifics of which Paula left out when recounting the evening to the cops.

The girls were almost evenly matched on the pool table, but by the end Aimee still had a solid purple four remain-ing when Paula sunk the eight. Aimee picked up the cue ball that betrayed her, held the weight of it in her palm for a moment, and returned it to the table. Paula went to the bar to pay for another game and Aimee stepped out for a cigarette. She never came back. Not seven and a half minutes later. Not an hour later. Not a week later. That cue ball was the last object anyone saw her touch.

Forty-eight hours into Aimee's absence, search parties bled into the fields. Inky silhouettes of police and locals blotted through farmland and car parks downtown, behind dumpsters, through our old high school football field, and along the riverbank veiled in honeysuckle. Volunteers sifted Sheep Pond with long sticks, pant legs rolled up to the knees, everyone praying, deep in their thudding hearts, that their sticks would not make contact with some firm, unknowable object. Maybe those wishes were heard, somewhere—they found nothing.

Paula spun that night at Rockyside endlessly in her head like a carousel, the same gaudy ponies coming back around over and over. *Oh god,* she kept thinking, *what if a stupid conversation about ferrets is the last thing my sister and I ever talk about?*

Last... That word was her darkest secret thought, tucked under a thousand blankets, locked in a Russian nesting doll of vaults: *last.* The unfathomable, the unspeakable, the impossible, needling notion that Aimee might be dead.

∽

Spell to Locate a Missing Person

YOU WILL NEED:

- *the last object the Missing Person touched before vanishing*

- a *"sacrifice"* (Consider a melon or grapefruit with a face drawn on it. Be creative!)
- a *ceremonial blade*
- a *coven of friends who love the Missing Person*
- a *full moon*

INTENT:

This spell will reveal the location of a Missing Person. Through the joint power of earth, moon, and symbolic sacrifice, the information you desire will manifest; once the sacrifice is offered, a map or visual clue revealing the location of the Missing will appear in the spilled "blood" (juice).

∽

We chose a real sacrifice because we wanted real results. The book itself may be tacky, but any act done with serious intent has the potential for success. As Paula nears the rooster, it falls still. One moment it's thrashing and the next it's completely calm, as if asleep. Its breath swells and recedes. Its empty eyes fill with the moon, no longer black but bony as bleached cotton. Paula pauses. Stefan's grip loosens, ever so slightly. The bird releases a wild caw, loud enough to ricochet off silo walls at the far end of Sheldon's Plot as the call shoots away through the dark. Then, Paula's knife slides into its chest—and the crowing deadens. Blood meets the soil. A pool. A well. A lake of ink. We wait for it to shape itself into a map, a sentence, an arrow, an image—anything. But anything never comes.

∽

Before we go further, I want to say that I'm not as good a friend as I seem. I don't mean I don't love Aimee. She's like family. I mean, shit, I trusted her to slam the door when I tied my first loose tooth to the knob. That's a blood bond. But even when you love a person, love them to the point of elaborate occultism, as the case may be, you can still make a mistake. You can still do a stupid thing. I'm saying this now because since Aimee's not here, I can't tell her myself, like I should have.

◊

I'm back at my old coffee shop job, the same one I had all through high school. I work the closing shift, which I like well enough because I'm alone for the final two hours, so I can play any music I want without coworkers judging my taste. Plus, I don't have to split tips. At half past ten I turn the sign to WICKED CLOSED! and dump what's left in the coffee urns into the sink. I've already put the cookies back in their plastic tubs and bundled the zucchini bread in cling wrap. Usually I'd steal a few slices for the road, if only out of minimum-wage spite, but my appetite hasn't been the same since Aimee went missing. All that's left is to take the trash into the back and count the change drawer.

With a garbage bag full of wet coffee grounds and milky napkins in hand, I head toward the stockroom. It's always a haven back there—hushed and cool. The ice machine makes little plinking sounds as it churns new cubes into the barrel and the milk fridge hums. I heave the trash into its plastic bin before taking the next day's cash drawer out of its hiding place in the refrigerator, sitting on a milk crate to count it up. The coins are chilled, and somehow feel smoother when cold like this. I like counting the nickels best, little glinting moons. *Moon. Sheldon's Plot. The rooster and the rooster's body and wherever its crowing went when the silence came. Aimee. Aimee, and the endless, endless places she might be.*

Something clicks against the storeroom window, just above my head. *Tap. Tap. Tap*, like a metronome. It's too loud to be a branch from one of the lilac bushes that sometimes scratches the pane when wind kicks up, yet too quiet for a knocking fist. *Tink. Tink.* I climb up on the milk to peek out.

Perched on the sill, illuminated by streetlights, is the rooster. Its wound is matted with dirt and husk, its beak drumming against glass. "Mother," it says, "let me in."

There are times to do as told and there are times to do the opposite. Which category this falls under, I can't say. But I can say that my hands decide for me. They spirit to the window like two dark birds reaching toward kin. They hoist it open. The rooster tumbles in.

"Thank you, Mother. It is so very cold out there, colder than any winter. I am grateful for shelter." Summer air sighs through the open window. It's muggy and warm. My heart gallops, unbridled, and for a moment my thoughts stray to Elijah, the pony Aimee and I learned to ride when we were nine or ten, how he tried to buck me off whenever I took to the saddle. Now my own pulse tries to do the same.

"Tell me, Mother—have you a dish of water, a needle, and thread? I am split open and I must be mended."

"I'm not . . . your mother," I say to the dead rooster.

"Ah yes, little Mother, but did you not read aloud from the book that birthed me here? The first book, one might say—for dying is so very like being born, and the book of my death turns out to be that, too, of my birth. Now fetch what I asked and clean my dying out. Death is such an unsightly accessory and I always wish to look my best." He puffs up his chest. A lick of bone shows through the gap.

Again, my hands move. They take a clean dish towel down from the shelf and fill a paper coffee cup with water, then set to cleaning the gash. Once it's as good as I can get it, I take a sewing needle and thread from the kit we keep near the paper towel stock. I don't know how to stitch a body. I have never held a shivering animal in my lap and pressed a needle into it. I hesitate.

"Please, Mother, close me. Imagine I am only a pocket-book that won't stay shut. Fabric. Your favorite purse with the roses on the side that you mended after the dog tore it with its teeth."

How did it know about that?

What else does it know?

"Please, Mother."

I stitch the rooster shut. It feels nothing like sewing a handbag.

∽

That night, I dream that a cornfield covers the whole town. I dip through it trying to find a way out, but there is no way out—just green in all directions. There are other people in the corn, too, mostly people we'd gone to high school with, but Jodie from my dorm back at Bard is there, too, and a few kids from my classes. When I ask them what they're doing in Johnsbury, Jodie says, "Looking for Aimee." Everyone is harvesting ears of corn and tearing them open with their teeth. I figure I should do the same. The ear I pick is plump and heavy and has a thin gold zipper on the side like a monarch chrysalis. When I rend it open, a tiny Aimee is tucked inside. She's naked and curled up tight like a new baby. "Look!" I shout. "I found her!" A few folks gather around to see. "No, that's not her," someone says. I realize that there are miniature Aimees inside everyone's ears of corn, sleeping or rubbing their eyes or combing their hair in their doll-like fingers. My Aimee sits up inside her husk and looks right at me.

"You should have been better," she says. I can feel her tiny heartbeat in the palm of my hand.

∽

My phone buzzes me out of the dream. It's Stefan; he doesn't bother saying hello.

"You saw it, too, didn't you?"

"Saw what?" My mind is still hazy with sleep. When I close my eyes, cornstalks silhouette in rows.

"The rooster told me it saw you at work, that you helped it. Is it true? Did you see it? Jesus, Molly, tell me I'm not the only one who saw this thing."

Waking up is the worst part of every day, because for a few seconds, I don't remember that Aimee is missing. I'm only aware of white light lapping at the floor and the heaviness of my own body. Then, the remembering comes. It's like a macabre *"Last week on [insert campy '90s monster show here]..."* where everything awful is compacted into one quick flash. Except I don't have superpowers or the ass to pull off pleather pants, and this is my real life, and my best friend is still gone.

"Did it call you Mother?" I ask Stefan.

"What?"

"The chicken, it called me Mother." This time he doesn't correct me, remind me that it's a rooster. The line goes quiet. "Stefan? You there?"

"It called me Oh My Darling."

"It . . . what?"

"Oh My Darling."

I laugh. I can't help it.

"It said it was because of how I held it . . . when it died. Like a lover." He sounded tired. More tired than I've ever heard him.

"Oh . . . that's fucked."

"We need to get Paula," he says. "Now."

On the drive over, I try not to think about being held by Stefan. The rooster is right. It does feel a bit like dying.

∽

The two of us meet in front of Paula and Aimee's house and enter through the garage door. The front entrance was fixed up at least three years ago and painted a devil-may-care cherry red, but we still use the back out of habit. We squeeze past a rusted tractor bloating in the middle of the floor, and I offer my hand to Stefan to help him climb over a crate of tools. He doesn't take it—just hoists himself past me and into the main part of the house. He's careful not to touch me as he passes, even lightly.

Usually, the girls' dad, Gary, would be in the living room playing the cello or trying to snare one of us into a debate about the legitimacy or lack thereof of homeopathic medicine. Not driving up and down Route 2 for twelve hours a day calling his daughter's name. When Aimee was born and he gave her that name, he never meant for it to be howled like this—again and again into the pitiless woods.

We pass through the hollow house. Paula's room is empty, but we can hear someone moving in Aimee's room at the end of the hall, the door ajar.

For a moment—hope.

"Paula?" Stefan calls.

"I'm in here!" she calls back.

The hope cracks.

Paula sits on Aimee's bed, her sister's infamous turquoise party dress (the one Aimee says makes her feel "like a mermaid who drowns sailors in cocktail punch") drooped over one knee. She's snipping it into penny-sized pieces with a pair of pinking shears, which pile into a soft heap in her lap. The rooster is perched beside her. He looks healthier than he did last night at the café. His tail feathers geyser into a blue arch, his crown ruby red and polished. Even his chest is handsome as a ripe peach. As Paula clips another piece of fabric loose, she gives it to the rooster, who takes it in his beak and swallows it. We watch Paula continue this way—feeding Aimee's dress to the rooster, scrap by scrap. Each time he eats another piece, his feathers slick a shade brighter.

Stefan reacts first, snatching the dress from Paula. It makes a whooshing sound as it rustles out of her grip. Stefan looks like he's about to cry, or punch a hole in the wall.

"This isn't yours," he barks. Aimee had worn that dress to our graduation. She and Stefan had flounced through the after-party bold as popped champagne, slow dancing next to a pyre of burning textbooks, making out in the swimming pool while that dress' sequins shot out sparks in a bright cascade.

"It's okay," Paula assures us. "He's helping. We're going to find her."

The rooster preens its glinting feathers.

"Hello, Mother. Hello, Oh My Darling. The Butcheress has been feeding me well, and I am much better dressed now for company. No more death sullying my fine features. Don't you agree?" He puffs up for us, looking more like a circus tent than a dead rooster.

"Do you know where our friend is?" I ask him.

"Of course. I am dead. The dead know everything."

"Is she okay?"

"I will not make proclamations; I would not want to be viewed as *cocky*." He wrenches into a bray at the pun, which sounds more like an ungreased door than jollity.

"But, sweethearts, I hunger. Feed me that which I crave and I will be able to give you all you seek. I can hear your dear one's longing bristle. Her shape, a shadow cast on the sundial of my tongue. I taste her motion. Her heart, a billiards game with the eight ball hovering midair, refusing to fall. Do you recall her hands, how they twitch into fever when anxious? I feel them sprinting through my blood, for what am I if not a river for the lost to travel through? You have built me for this. You with your knife, with your hexes, with your ropes, your bloodlettings. Sweet ones, children of my death-birth, you cannot know the pang of this hunger. Feed me from the grain stock of her living—and I will lead you to her."

We do the rooster's bidding. Feed it clothes still smoky with the musk of Aimee's skin. Water from a glass with lipstick on the rim. Black jelly from a mascara tube and a single snagged eyelash. Clots of hair stuck in her comb or slapped to the shower wall. We feed him photographs, diary keys, lime-green fishnet stockings, a garter belt with a flask at the hip. The delicacies grow larger, and the rooster's gullet widens and widens, an unhinged famine—whole poetry books and high-top sneakers and bottles of glitter sipped down easy as aspirin.

When the rooster finally stops eating, all of Aimee's most precious objects are gone. The room has been thieved of its Aimee-ness, her essence absorbed into the bird's body. He remains the same size as ever, while the walls sport lost-tooth gaps where band posters once hung. The concert is over. The crowd has all gone home, stumbled in clusters off the walls and sills and out from dresser drawers, straight into the rooster's beak.

If Aimee were missing before . . . she is twice as absent now.

The creature pecks a last stray bobby pin off the carpet before settling, his legs vanishing under a blob of feathers. He wheezes inward as if readying to speak, and I think (I can't help it, how could I help it?), *This will be the day I learn my best friend is dead.* And for a moment, I would do anything, truly anything, to keep him from talking.

But he doesn't talk. The rooster shuts his eyes and sinks low into his plumage. He falls into a terrible kind of sleep. No shaking, no fury, no tugging of wings or plucking of feathers will wake him. He is loose and breathless, head drooped to one side, the knife wound on his chest visible again—once more a slain animal on an altar. And every artifact of Aimee we had left remains stolen by a ravenousness that we, ourselves, have conjured.

Aimee, I heard once that everybody dies twice—once when their heart stops, and again when their name is spoken for the last time. But there is another sort of dying in between, a *crueler* death: when those you love begin to make choices they would never make if you were there. If you were alive. Things that would be thoughtless, brutal even, but in your absence, become benign. Like giving away your clothes. Or removing the flurries of magazine clippings you carefully curated across your bedroom walls.

Isn't it strange, how the rules change so fast? How an act that would be unacceptable one moment becomes instantly harmless, as soon as the burden of ownership is lifted? Like how I intercept Stefan in the hall. How I lean against him until he cannot help but harden at the heat of this new body. How I bring his hands to my waist and bristle into chills as they slip under my shirt, as they glance over my breasts, just barely making contact. How I kiss him. And what of the guilt that follows? That must be my hope speaking, for what is there to feel guilt over unless you are, in fact, alive and returning to us? And then—then, there is the other sort of hope. The awful spark of hope that says, *This is allowed now. I'm doing nothing wrong.* In that dark hope is where the crueler death resides.

HOMEBODY

BRICK, WOOD, GLASS, WOOD screws, cement. These are the makings of a house. The makings of a body are different, softer and less precise. A house is not a body and a body is not a house. That's the way of things. Of course it is.

～

It takes a great deal of time to unload all the boxes. You should have hired movers—saving the money hardly seems worth it now as you heave the back end of a sofa up a narrow stairwell. By the time you and Marlow finish lugging your belongings into the new house, it's evening. You are proud and you are tired, and proud of your tiredness, because it means you accomplished something. Marlow says, *This place is going to serve us well.* You think that's a funny way for him to put it. You would have said it the other way around. You put on a white apron and drag a broom back and forth along the kitchen floor and ask the house, *What can we do for you now? Do you feel beautiful enough? Do you feel strong?* You will be good to the house, and in turn, the house will be good to you.

∽

The first moment you saw Marlow, you didn't love him. Then in the second moment, you did. You were working at a gallery, and he had driven from three states away to attend an opening in which his latest paintings were being shown. Initially he'd seemed *too* handsome, his jaw too sharp, his blond curls catching light inhumanely. You rarely were drawn to perfect-looking men. But then, that second moment descended as soon as Marlow began speaking about his work, some lovely mirage rising from his throat and from the shapes on the canvases behind him. You had planned to leave after your shift ended, just lingering enough for a free glass of wine and a napkin full of brie, but you stayed all night—through early waves of gallery chatter, then later, then later still, until the visitors had all filtered out. You invited Marlow over to your apartment, and he made some joke about how you were too easy, or maybe how he was too easy, and the truth was you were both easy as hell, and no one minded.

You drove to him on the weekends or he drove to see you. At his shows and lectures, you took secret satisfaction in the skinny women who hung back, waiting for a chance to flatter the artist, handbags dangling from their elbows like fruit bats. They wanted him. You had him.

He couldn't move away. Naturally he couldn't, he had his teaching job, and a community that respected him.

You liked working at the gallery, but the gig was nothing special. Not like Marlow was special. So when the time came, by default, you went to him.

∾

On your third night in the new house, you and Marlow host a party. Every room still feels new, like a little cake yet to be sliced. When you pass between them, you balance on tiptoe so as not to disturb the freshness of it all.

Before the guests arrive, you put on a slim black dress and your brightest red lipstick: Red Revolution. You kiss the mirror, leaving a petal of a print behind, and you line your eyes with kohl. You feel like a kitchen fire. A bright, hungry thing. Come nightfall, you'll wear high heels within your own damn home and you'll meet Marlow's friends who'll ask you about your own paintings, which you've hung in the entrance hall and the living room, and you'll nod and say, *Yes, well, I was experimenting with deconstructing the feminine, with nonrepresentational images of womanhood*, and they will all be very impressed, not to mention mesmerized by your tits in the slim black dress, and the fire in you will bloom and bloom and bloom in this new place.

In the kitchen, Marlow is readying the bar. He lines up liquor bottles like a regiment of toy soldiers. You slither into his arms and try to kiss him, but he pulls away. *I don't want to get that lipstick on me,* he says, leaning out of your reach. *Babe, your lips are so pretty when you leave them their natural color.* He kisses the top of your head. He's right—the scarlet feels glaring as a hydrant, or an alarm going off. It's too much.

Returning to the bathroom, you decide Blushing Berry will do instead. It's subtler. Plus, it is almost the precise shade of the bathroom tile, which pleases you. It makes you feel closer to the house. Kindred. Wiping the ruby away with a wad of tissue, the flame on your mouth snuffs out.

So you're Marlow's girlfriend! A woman who introduces herself as Rebecca pushes through the crowd and extends her hand to shake, spilling her drink a little on your new carpet in the process. The party is running smoothly. You're busy meeting people, one after another, a cacophony of faces. Some, Marlow's told you about, and you revel in knowing contraband gossip about people who believe you to be a stranger. For example, you know that Marlow has slept with a number of the women here, Rebecca among them. You don't mind this; they've all known each other a long time, for much longer than you've known Marlow. You're happy to be integrating.

I adore his work, Rebecca croons. *Honestly, I am completely infatuated with his Green Desert series. I would kill for that kind of talent—wouldn't you?* Your favorite of your own paintings, Woman Bathes in Molten Gold, hangs beside Rebecca's left shoulder. You consider pointing it out, but decide against it.

I'm sorry, Rebecca says, *what did you say your name was again?* You start to tell her you haven't said your name was anything, yet, but before you can, she darts off to Marlow, leaving you to gaze at the lovely periwinkle of your living room wall. In your periphery, you see him brush his hand down Rebecca's lower back. She laughs.

How delightful to be periwinkle. Always a sigh to look at, as if living in a cloud of perfume. You decide your next painting will feature the shade heavily. Woman Bathes in Periwinkle.

∽

You are drunk in the shower. The guests have vanished, and so has the rest of your fifth Manhattan. You bury shampoo in your hair with your hands, and when you wash it out, little blue flakes rinse out, too. Periwinkle paint, nearly enough to fill a highball glass. Aghast, you scurry, pink and towel-less, to the living room and fling on the lights. You scour the wall for cracks, or chips, or any evidence of decay. But no. The wall is smooth and taut as a hotel bed.

∽

Entry Hall: five bronze coat hooks; olive walls
Kitchen: white linoleum floor; white cabinets; robin's-egg trim
Living Room: built-in bookcase; hardwood floor; two east-facing floor-length windows with fat muntins; periwinkle walls; ivory trim
Central Hall: a marble placed on one end will not roll but remain dutifully and levelly in place
Bathroom: berry walls; shower; toilet; mirror (reflection errs on flattering)
Bedroom: ocean of bed where you unpeel Marlow like an artichoke, leaf by leaf (does the bed have edges? unproven); closet inlaid into southern wall, illuminated by an ungloved bulb, flickering, flickering.

∽

You hang a primed canvas on the studio wall, already stretched over its skeleton. You paint it periwinkle. Over the periwinkle, you add a window, but the window won't stop looking at you, so you paint over it again. In its place, you press your palms into the wet. Then you walk into the living room and hold up your hands. You almost cannot tell where the edge lies between the walls and you.

Marlow's paintings are roughly three times the size of yours, so most of the studio is reserved for him. You wish he had more room to work. It's too cramped for both of you—plus, he likes to paint to music, so the radio is always on. You prefer silence. Otherwise you can't hear your paintings when they tell you what they need. Maybe you can give him the studio and set your materials elsewhere. When you ask Marlow what he thinks of your Woman Bathing in Periwinkle, he asks, *Where is the woman?* which makes no sense, because you are standing right there.

∽

Your favorite part of the house: a perfect rectangle of sunlight that buzzes on the hardwood floor in the midafternoon. Once, you took off all your clothes and curled up naked in it like a cat.

Your second favorite part of the house is the little trap door over the kitchen sink. It's too high to reach, and has no latch or knob. You like it because it could lead to anything—to the sky, to a secret room, to a whole second house upturned on top of your own. Your favorite theory is that it's a portal leading back to your last apartment. If you're ever on the lam, or things go south with Marlow, you'll just hoist a ladder into the kitchen sink and climb back to where you came from. Until then, you hope no one ever opens it. As long as no one opens it, it still can lead to everything.

It is the twenty-third day in the new house. You haven't found a job in town yet, so you spend a lot of time lying upside down on the couch. You like putting your legs up against the back of the sofa with your own back on the seat, imagining the wall is the floor and the floor is the wall. It's important to not get stuck on one perspective. If you get stuck on one perspective, things get stale, and then you may not notice the ornate ornamentation inlaid into the ceiling fan. Other activities include learning to shuffle cards in elaborate, showy formation like a blackjack dealer; sewing new curtains for every window in the house; thinking about painting and getting ready to paint and then not painting anything. Here's a secret about artists: most of them would rather be doing anything else on the planet than making their art. You find this knowledge comforting as you scrub the counters down even though they are already clean. There are so many hours to fill in a day. Time in this city works differently than in your old city. It expands like over-chewed steak the longer you gnaw on it.

Marlow is away most of the time. He lectures to undergrads during the day. Some nights he returns very, very late. One evening, before he gets back, you climb into a new dress and then take it off and then put it on again.

There are many bronze buttons trickling down the front seam. The process takes ages. But the problem is, you can never tell what Marlow will like. Maybe he'll river his hands along your hips and kiss you and lay you down on the hallway floor to pop open the buttons one by one by one. Or maybe he'll say, offhand, *Huh, I never noticed your ass is sort of . . . crooked? That dress really points it out. Not an insult, just an observation.* You take the dress off again. In its place you put on the periwinkle one with the long sleeves that Marlow says is his favorite.

You wonder if your dresses know, already, which one of them will be worn on the day when Marlow inevitably leaves you. If even back in the factory, while the serger chewed each hem shut, the fabric already had every future day imprinted on it. Every memory yet to be born could be as much a part of the garment as the dye, the thread, the little white tag at the neck.

Thinking like this makes you anxious to the point of nausea. Indigestion. Erratic pulse. The only thing that calms you down before Marlow comes home is a trick that Marlow taught you. You envision a small glowing light at the top of your head, and let it slowly, slowly scan down the length of your body. Past your hairline. Your eyebrows. Your eyelids, closing. The cold tip of your nose, your lips. But when you reach your throat, you start to cough. The coughing won't stop. In the bathroom, you hack into a handkerchief until whatever is in there shakes loose with a final choke. You look into the cloth, and find you have coughed up a small, brass key.

You try the key on the front door. It fits.

∽

You aren't stupid. You know what this looks like. A woman uproots her life and moves to a new city for a man. Is known not by her name, but as this guy's girlfriend. The man himself is beautiful, yes, and soft, and tender in his way, but absent somehow. He speaks mindlessly. He's a little too into himself. Horribly, it's very easy to be in love with someone you don't particularly like. The woman loves him the way a honeybee loves the sting—fevered for contact, willing to tug its own guts out in the process. You aren't an idiot. This isn't a good look on anyone. But isn't part of free will getting to say fuck it and follow your passion anyway? So fuck it. At least you have a beautiful house that sways and sways and whispers to you in a low, lilting song.

~

Marlow runs hot in the night and you run cold. You let him sleep with the air-conditioning on, but only if he lets you fall asleep pressed up against him. In the middle of the night, you wake shivering and untouched, your sweetheart on the far edge of the bed. All the windows, open. You rise to close them, fuzzy with sleep, and as you snap the sliding glass down, you pinch your thumb in the lock. A sharp inhale. A yelp so small, Marlow never even hears. You run your finger under cold water in the bathroom. The nail shimmers, a black lobe of blood underneath. Looking closer, you see a tiny AC unit wedged between your thumbnail and cuticle—such a small cube you can hardly tell what it is at first. You tuck your thumb into your palm, but it blows and blows all night. The chill keeps you awake for hours.

〜

You've seen it before—women becoming houses. A girl you roomed with in college is now a lovely Victorian cottage with scalloped trim. Your Aunt Livia transformed halfway into a Gothic revival with a mansard roof before recovering and moving to Barbados instead. Knuckles traded for polished mahogany balustrades, eyes brimming with thick wooden sills, shutters swinging from shoulder blades like rigid wings. Sometimes it happens slowly. Sometimes all at once.

It was shocking, the first time you saw a woman turned into a house. You were a young girl then, seven or eight. You were on a family trip to Maine, mansion-ogling by the shore. Looming residences with towering cupolas and widow's walks lined the waterside. Wealth on parade. One house at the end of the lane had a trellis vining up the side that you itched to climb, but as you drew closer, you realized something was *wrong* with the house. It was alive. You don't know how you knew it was alive—it looked no different from the other houses—but you were sure of it. When you looked up into the cold windows, the outline of a woman scattered from pane to pane, refracting and warping before dissolving into the walls. Later, you asked your mother about the house. "Oh, sweetie," she said. "You don't have to worry about that. You have a good head on your shoulders." You weren't sure what that had to do with the alive house, but you didn't ask about it again.

It isn't a new phenomenon, but there remains contention among doctors as to what makes women lose their human bodies and become houses. Certain camps within the medical community claim that it isn't an actual occurrence at all, but merely psychosomatic. A feminine overreaction. Pure drama. But you've begun waking in the night to the sound of a doorbell ringing in place of your own breath. You've found little knobs on you that weren't there before—a light switch behind your left ear that blinds you when flicked, a latch behind your knee that swings open a small door, putting all your dumb-waiter sinews and muscles on display. You've felt a breeze pass through the open windows of your body, brushing the curtains aside.

☙

Your sister is the only person you tell about your house-becoming. When you call her, it's pouring rain outside, and your right elbow has sprung a leak where the storm is getting in. You put a saucepan under it to catch the water.

You don't have to let this happen, she says.

Let? you think. *Did I let this happen? When did I decide to do this?*

Have you heard about that awful procedure women are subjecting themselves to? It's very popular in London, and parts of Scandinavia apparently.

What procedure? you ask.

It's a surgery, your sister says, *where women who are partial builds will have themselves converted full-on. Speed up the process. It's awful. Disgusting.*

Come on, you say, *I wouldn't do something like that. You know I wouldn't.*

I just want you to know that you're playing with something dangerous, she says. *People can get carried away with this stuff.*

I want you to be sure you're thinking about what you really want.

Your sister asks if you're happy this is happening, or afraid, and you try to answer, but then the power goes out, and your voice stops working along with it.

∾

You and Marlow visit his parents for Christmas, and you can't figure out what to wear. You haven't left home in weeks. Plus, none of your old dresses are flattering now that your curves have been replaced with sharp, geometric angles.

My mom's pretty traditional, says Marlow. *Maybe don't wear that one shirt. You know, the strapless one. I don't want her to think you're . . . I don't know, promiscuous or something.*

You settle for wrapping yourself in Tyvek siding, which not only appears exceedingly modest for Marlow's mother's sake, but also keeps the rain from seeping into your newly lain plywood roof. You can't wait for the tin to grow in.

You're beautiful, says Marlow when he sees you, coated head to toe.

∾

When you get to Marlow's parents' house, his mother is halfway through baking a blueberry pie.

My boys love blueberry pie! I always have one ready when they get home, she says. Clouds of flour spirit up from her hands. She's wearing an apron that reads MAMA, WIFE, BLESSED LIFE.

Is this a joke? you think. You realize she is not joking.

Marlow eats three slices of blueberry pie. You aren't hungry. Your appetite hasn't been the same since you started to transform into a house. You aren't even sure what houses eat. Earlier that week, you'd googled, "What do houses eat?" which only yielded a series of negative Yelp reviews for a truck-stop diner called EatHaus. "Worst hash browns I've ever had. I will never return." "They should call this place FeetHaus." One review just said, "I am devastated."

You ask Marlow's mother if she has any favorite stories of Marlow as a little boy. She tells you a story you already know, in part. Marlow was nine or ten. All he wanted was a pair of Rollerblades, but his mother forbade it. He was too small, and they were too dangerous. Never one to be deterred, he snuck out to the skate park with a pocketful of Hot Wheels cars and a spool of fishing wire. He strapped the cars to the bottoms of his sneakers and plummeted into the half pipe at full speed. Of course he fell. Head split open on the ramp. Fourteen stitches across the chin. A cracked tooth. *He was always so imaginative,* said Marlow's mother, *so resourceful. And so impulsive! Mar hated brushing his teeth after that. I had to do it for him for years—till he was almost twelve! Oh, he hates when I tell people that.* Marlow cringed. *But my little boy always did need someone there to take care of him.* She winks at you, pats your arm. *He still does!*

∿

You continue with your Woman Bathing in Periwinkle series. Originally, you'd imagined five canvases, growing continuously more saturated with color as they progressed. However, Marlow's been working on a

larger scale lately, canvases six or seven times the size
of yours, and he asked if you'd be willing to work small
for a while. The studio isn't large enough for you to fit
more. So instead of your planned series, you create each
new work on the same canvas, every painting layered on
top of the one before it. It's getting harder to hold the
paintbrush, now that your hands have turned into sliding screen doors.

Marlow is unsure of his work. He fears it might be terrible. He fears no one will understand the symbolic juxta-
position of saguaro green with cucumber green. He fears
he will vanish into obscurity, his work abandoned in a
junkyard and his name lost to time. You promise him he
won't, because you will call his name out daily and carve
it into the walls of this house and neighbors' houses and
you won't stop hollering until his work is safe. *You're
brilliant,* you say, stroking his hair. You've had this conversation before. Marlow's doubt is an ouroboros swal-
lowing its tail, always coming back around. These are the
times you feel boldest. These are the times he needs you.
I wouldn't be here with you if you weren't talented, you say. *I
only date geniuses. It's my base rule.* And so Marlow laughs,
and you laugh with him, hiccuping up a grandfather
clock in the process.

✒

After your pubic hair falls out and electrical wiring
sprouts in its place, you start to wonder if this is such a
bad thing after all. Being a house could be useful, in its
way. It will be easier to settle into a new city if you are,
well, *part* of the neighborhood. And it can help you care
for Marlow in all the ways you yearn to nurture him. It's

not like you have anything better to do. You could try this for a while. And then, if you weary of being residential, you'll just turn back. Reversing the process is rare, it's true—but Aunt Livia did it, didn't she? You could, too. Easy. Parts of it are fun, even. Like whenever you make a phone call, you don't even have to dial—one of your eyelashes is hooked up to the telephone pole down the street. All you do is blink. Maybe you'll like being a house. Maybe you'll like being a house more than you like being a person.

༄

Look, you say, tilting your head to the side. *It would make a perfect studio, wouldn't it? I cleared it out for you, if you want to use it.*

Marlow presses his eye up to your ear and peeks inside. There's a room just past your eardrum, twice the size of Marlow's old painting studio. You've put a stool in the corner and painted the walls white, and you've pounded a row of nails across the far wall for hanging canvases.

I chose it for the good lighting, you say, tugging on your earlobe so more sunglow can fill the room. *I want you to have it. Use it for whatever you want.*

༄

You love him fiercely. You paint his portrait on the wall of the new house, only to realize you were painting on your own shoulder the whole time. You find a wood screw behind one ear. Marlow slaps your ass as you fuck, and he gets a splinter. One night, you reach for the refrigerator door, and your hand melts into the handle. This is all normal. You are becoming hospitable. Call it a virus or a happening. Don't ask what triggers a body to become host, how a skeleton can step aside to make room for guests.

There is a hollowing-out. A decluttering. No man will sleep in a storage closet, and you were so full, once, of furniture. Part of you recalls a difference in semantics between she and it, between house and lover, but you forget the distinctions. You are unstoppable in your offerings. Your hair is cropped, just the way Marlow likes it, sloped so the rain slides off into the gutter, a tin-roofed cut.

∾

Three months in the new house. Marlow sleeps with another woman. He tells you about it two weeks later. *I was scared,* he said, *I was scared of what you would say. It was terrible anyway, I made a mistake.* He starts to cry. *I'm a horrible boyfriend. Do you think I'm horrible?*

Shh, you say, looping the balcony of your arm around him. *Shhhh, darling, it's okay. You'll be okay. You aren't horrible, you're good, a good pers—* You're cut off as your throat fills with chimney soot.

∾

Marlow isn't sleeping well. The mattress is too soft, he says. Too giving. He's been sleeping on the couch. One morning, you follow him there, your hardwood feet clacking against the floor, and seduce him. It's only a few minutes before he pauses. *We should stop,* he says. *I'm not present right now. I was thinking of someone else.* He's still inside you.

Why do women in movies always wrap the bedsheet around themselves when they get up to go to the bathroom? You wrap yourself up like a moth in a cocoon and walk to the kitchen. It's harder to wrap elegantly than the movie women make it look. You keep stepping on one corner and tripping.

Hey, where are you going? Marlow asks.

You put the kettle on to boil, then drop a chamomile tea bag into a chipped pink mug. The water pours out cloudy with steam. Above the sink, the little trap door hovers, leading upward, into everywhere, into the sky, into another life.

In the next room, you can hear Marlow breathing. He's slipping away from you. He is slipping away.

∽

The next day, you make an appointment to undergo the surgery. It's nothing drastic. They'll simply expedite a process already in motion. Make things official. The procedure is quick, and the anesthetic strong. You sleep and you do not dream.

When you awake in your wheeled hospital bed, you're complete. A mirror is held up in front of you and you sigh a cloud of periwinkle breath. The surgeon and his carpentry team have done fine work. You look just like the real estate photos: a redbrick chimney with a steel chimney pot juts from what was once your left temple, and three dormer windows have been installed in your hairline. Your scalp is shingled, with a skylight to one side. In your throat, a set of French doors. Eaves are tucked below your breasts, your ribs removed and replaced with marble columns. When you peek inside the open window where your navel used to be, you find yourself clean and gleaming and empty. They even built on an addition to Marlow's studio. Anyone would be lucky to live in you.

～

Six months in the new house. You are the new house. Marlow says a word you do not recognize one night, and you ask him what it means. He says this word is your name. You are a bold, creaking thing. *Come,* you call, *wander through me! I am wide enough to contain a whole other person's life. Come through the hallway, lie in my spot of sunlight! Sleep in the bed I cradle in my mouth! Stay as long as you like. Let me hold you, and hold you, and hold you.*

～

House is the new house is the body is a thing is now empty enough. So big you, house, fill the foundation. Language, harder now. Once, you knew. Once, you girl. House. Forget.

～

Inside is a man. He is piling his clothes on the bed. He is filling suitcases. There is a moving truck on your foot and you try to toss it off but it does not toss. The man is dragging a sofa down your ribs. It is raining or you are raining or the faucet has been left on too long. The man turns off every light switch in you as he leaves.

In the kitchen, a tiny trap door hovers above the sink. You tongue it on the roof of your mouth. It's jammed. You push. You push. You try to shake the little door loose.

A Haunted Calendar

DAY 1 WHEN THOMAS opens the cabinet, he finds his sister inside. "Where are we, Thomas?" she asks. Thomas takes out a cereal bowl & a box of Cheerios. "Where are we, Thomas?" Thomas closes the cabinet.

Day 2 There is a party full of ghosts. They are doing keg stands & smoking Pall Malls on the back porch. One ghost kisses another ghost by the bathroom door. Someone calls the cops on them, but when the cops get there, they only find an empty house. The party goes all century.

Day 3 Layla didn't like to leave the bench. The bench faced Weatherhead Pond & was made of good, thick oak. The bench bore Layla's name on a metal plaque, along with a date. Layla liked to trace the letters with her little blue fingers & cough up water.

Day 4 Mary found the box in the trunk of her car, closed with a padlock. Even bolt cutters wouldn't open it. But sometimes, she would whisper into the box & sometimes the box would whisper back.

Day 5 When I say I love you, I mean I reach for you. When I say I reach for you, I mean you went out to buy a bottle of gin & didn't come back. When I say you didn't come back, I mean I woke last night with you in my bed, but my hands slipped right through you.

Day 6 Ghost (noun):
The suspended sensation of watching a wineglass tilt off a table's edge—knowing it will shatter, but being powerless to stop it.

Day 7 After the war, we waited in the orchard for the apples to swell—but this year, the trees bore no fruit; only little white scarves, surrendering again & again in the autumn wind.

Day 8 Ghost (verb):
To write all your old boyfriend's names in the fog on a bathroom mirror.

————

Day 9 A corn-husk doll. A familiar song you whistle without noticing. A pile of peaches rotting, uneaten, on the table. A journal with the pages blacked out. The same song, again. A name that sounds like yours. A name that doesn't.

Day 10 Ghost (verb):
When you think someone is smiling & waving at you so you wave back but they are actually waving at someone behind you wait no they are not smiling, they are yelling, they are pointing desperately behind you, they are crying now, you turn around &

Day 11 Did you know that a teardrop is nothing but a small, wet ghost? Whenever you cry, an onslaught drips free to wreak lord knows what mischief. Remember when you wept in front of your beloved, & they looked so very frightened? Well—now you know why.

Day 12 Ghost (noun):
A letter you write but never send.

Day 13 Ghost (noun):
Her toothbrush left in the cup even months later. A T-shirt you will not wash. A profile you've muted, but check daily anyway, you idiot. A regret.

Day 14 At first, Alika didn't mind the ghost. It just made mismatched pairs of her socks, ate the stale ends of bread, wriggled around like a worm in the bottom of her soup bowls. But then the baby went missing.

Day 15 Little frog, prince of darkness, opens its mouth to ribbit but no ribbit comes out. Instead: a rainstorm. An unlit lantern. A woman on her knees begging for forgiveness.

Day 16 Knock, knock.
Who's there?
Ghost.
Ghost who?
Ghost-ay on the couch; I don't want to sleep next to you tonight.

Day 17 If you say Bloody Mary into the mirror three times, a woman will appear. She will call you by your name. She will offer you a coupon book. This will seem like a good deal. It is NOT a good deal. Repeat: It is NOT a good deal. Turn away. Don't consider the two-liter Pepsi discount.

Day 18 A boy found a bicycle in the forest made of bones. When he rode it, the bones spoke. They told him how they died. They told him everything his friends whispered to each other when the boy was not around.

They told him terrible, beautiful secrets & the boy rode & rode.

Day 19 Fact: Ghosts say "Boo" because Abe Lincoln, the first ghost, tried to call out to his killer, Booth, but was stopped short by death.

Day 20 There is a door in the river. I opened it. I didn't open it. I'll never open it. I cannot stop opening it, again & again, every time I think of you, of where you've gone.

Day 21 A palm reader works in a nail salon. She reads futures for her customers as she works. One day, she paints the nails of a woman who has no lines on her hands at all. The salon worker quits her job. She moves to Cincinnati. On a kitchen hot plate, she singes her palms to blanks.

Day 22 Don't hitch a ride in the blue Chevy. It's been driving circles though this town since 1801. Back before pickups were invented. But if the driver leans out his window to offer you a Slim Jim, you're advised to accept. They're very good Slim Jims. Exemplary, devastating Slim Jims.

Day 23 An owl eats a small ghost thinking it is a field mouse. After that, he can hear all the little bone pellets talking to one another inside him, all day, all night.

———————

Day 24 You squeeze the shampoo bottle & a ghost falls out. It lathers into your hair. At work, all your colleagues compliment you on how shiny & healthy your hair looks. Thank you, you say. It flows in thick, red ringlets. Later that night, it falls out in clumps, until not a strand is left.

Day 25 Fact: Ghosts do not belong only to the dead. They belong to whatever is absent. A sweetheart. A misplaced key. A hometown you fled in a glinting jet plane while swearing never, never to return.

Day 26 Ruby sees her spectral double at the bodega, buying a large bag of cat food. Something is wrong, Ruby thinks. Terribly wrong. I do not own a cat.

Day 27 Cloven-Toe goes to the farmers' market. He samples the elderberry wine. He samples little cubes of cheese. Purple carrots. Garlic scapes. Cloven-Toe visits the young goats, penned in the back of a truck. He tells them their true names. When he leaves, the goats are trembling, trembling.

Day 28 To summon a ghost: 1. Shine the flatware until it glints so bright it stings. 2. Fill all silver spoons with honey. 3. Dust all knives with cake flour. 4. Dip the forks in salt and lick them clean. 5. Bury the flatware in the garden. Walk away. Never call home again. Let the ghost take your place.

Day 29 Yarra worked pumping gas all through high school. Into every gas tank, she slipped a little scrap of paper & on each paper she left a Revolution Red lipstick print from her own mouth. When the cars drove away, they took this bit of Yarra with them, without even knowing—past exit 6, past the town limits, past the horizon lipping over the edge of the world.

Day 30 When a ghost dies, it too produces a ghost. Half cello string, half X-Acto blade. Half tattoo, half firework. Half museum after dark, half catamount prowling deeper & deeper into the forest for prey.

Day 31 Ghost infestation? We can help! We'll leave violets to wilt on your pillow! We'll feed you full droppers of laudanum! We'll pluck your eyelashes one by one by one! Will this banish the ghosts? No! Nothing will banish the ghosts! Nothing will banish the ghosts! Nothing will banish the ghosts! Nothing wi

The Plums at the End of the World

CHAPTER ONE:
Harvest

In the goat woman's yard, a garden. In the garden, a tree. On the tree were plums unlike any fruit you've ever tasted. These plums appeared only when it rained. Each began as a simple water droplet dangling from the bough, which would blister into a harvest the size of a goat's heart. The plums were dark as blood and sweet as spun sugar and if the goat woman were to eat one, the world would end.

CHAPTER TWO:
Origins

Before the goat woman there was the goat woman's mother—a farm girl, clumsy with desire. Every pail of water she hauled to the barn arrived half empty, so fiercely her hands shook with wanting. It took her four or five tries to get the bit into the plow horse's mouth, an hour to milk a single cow. Her yearn was unyielding. It made her useless. It ruined her motions, seized each small ligament in her body and set them to untamed fluttering. The goat woman's mother lay awake each night in her itchy, hay-stuffed bed, staring at a pale stain on the ceiling. The stain took the shape of her desire. It was an unbearable shape, amorphous and swollen at the corners, a shape with no name and nothing to compare it to.

The goat woman's mother was young still, no more than fifteen, but already she knew that she must never resolve this wanting. She had seen others punished for much less. The previous summer, a girl she had schooled with had been caught naked in the river with the baker's son. They had nailed her earlobe to a wooden post in the square. Later, a boy cousin of hers had hidden a drawing of Eve in the Garden beneath his bedroom floorboard, and when his father found it, he sent the boy away to work the lumber camp. The boy returned with only three fingers, the rest lost to frostbite. The goat woman's mother knew the cost of want—and yet, she shook and shook and dreamt nightly of the farmhands who helped her father in the wheat fields. She would be a stalk of wheat, bending in their hands. She would be the rain that fell down the backs of their necks. Upon waking, the goat girl's mother wept with guilt.

She tried to cure herself. First, she prayed three days and nights without sleeping. But still, the wanting. Then, she chewed bitter dandelion root until her stomach was sore. But still, the wanting. She slapped her own knuckles with a willow switch, walked barefoot on sharp pebbles, bathed in the icy water of the creek until her lips turned blue. But still—the wanting remained.

One spring, the farm's finest goat gave birth to a healthy kid. He was all white, with a red-brown spot on the nose, and the goat woman's mother was tasked with his care. She loved the kid. She fed him blackberries from her palm and let him chew on the hem of her skirt. She taught him tricks the way you would a dog—fetch and come and play dead. And the kid grew into a strong, healthy animal.

One night, the goat woman's mother lay awake, shaking. She had watched one of the farmhands undress behind the silo when he thought no one was watching. It had thrown the girl into such distress that she feared she wouldn't survive. She was built of electricity, all static and heat, ready to burst into sparks. She went to the barn. The goat was tied to a post with a length of rope. She lay in the dust beneath it. And animals will do as instinct bids.

When the goat woman was born, it was clear to everyone what her mother had done. In accordance with the laws of Leviticus, the goat was brought before the goat woman's mother and slaughtered. The goat woman's mother was hanged.

And it was from this yearning and sorrow that the goat woman brayed into life.

CHAPTER THREE:
Testimonials

Pliny the Elder [1st century CE] (Natural History, Book 8, 76): It is said that goats can see at night just as well as they can by day; a diet of goat liver can restore sight in someone suffering night blindness. If a goat licks an olive tree the tree will become barren; the bite of a goat will kill a tree. Archelaus says that goats breathe through their ears instead of their nostrils, and always have a fever; this may be why they are so lively and hotter during mating.

Isidore of Seville [7th century CE] (Etymologies, *Book 12, 1:14-15): The goat (*hircus*) is a lascivious animal; it likes to butt heads and is always ready to mate. Because of its lust its eyes are slanted, from which it gets its name (*hirqui* are the corners of the eyes). The nature of goats is so hot that their blood can dissolve diamond.*

CHAPTER FOUR:
Childhood

When the goat woman was a small girl, her grandfather sold her to a Mister Pluvio of Mister Pluvio's Traveling House of Horrors. The man paid the goat girl's grandfather one hundred fifty dollars to take the goat girl away.

"Well aren't you a terrible creature," the impresario said when he first saw her. "A terrible, wonderful creature."

The House of Horrors displayed her nightly to an intimate, high-paying crowd of businessmen and politicians. She would sit upright in a folding metal chair and eat the labels off soup cans. She would hold up her cloven hooves and ask the audience to shake her hand. If you paid extra, you could touch one of two speckled horns, gleaming like snowflake obsidian, protruding from the goat girl's forehead. She winked her slivered pupils at the audience and bleated. Once in a while, the goat girl would feel the urge to nip her blunt teeth at a visitor, snapping off a fingertip or bit of arm flesh in the process. And because it made her more frightening, more danger-ous, Mister Pluvio never faulted her for this.

"Yes, little horror, yes," he whispered to her, dabbing flecks of blood from her chin after the curtains closed. "Lean into your monstrousness and you'll make us both very rich."

No one had ever encouraged the goat girl to embrace her animal side before. Back in her grandfather's house, she'd been hidden from the outside world. She was forced to wear a floppy straw hat at all times to cover her bud-ding horns. She wasn't allowed outside in full sunlight, or in any of the rooms with wide, east-facing windows, lest her full form be illuminated. She was permitted to eat only simple, human food like brown bread with salt. Once, her grandfather caught her chewing sod in the back meadow and forced her to sleep outside in the dirt for a month, though it was nearing winter.

"Either be a girl or be a beast, but you can't be both," her grandfather jeered. "Act like a beast? Then you'll live like a beast."

Weekly, a priest would come to splash holy water into her fur.

But at the House of Horrors, it was the opposite. The more animallike she acted, the more Mister Pluvio rewarded her. She would fail to lift a teacup delicately in her hooves and the crowd would howl. She would recite poetry and Shakespeare for the audience while buck-ing around her pen on all fours, and silver coins would rain into the enclosure. If she urinated in plain sight or kicked over the metal chair, Mister Pluvio would ensure an extra-large supper portion for her that night. She could be as beastly as she wished. In fact, if she erred too human, sitting too primly or combing her fur too neat, Mister Pluvio would adjust her to a slump and muss her long ears with dirt. In this way, she began to forget she was half girl at all.

"Why be a girl," cooed Mister Pluvio, "when you could be a terror?"

CHAPTER FIVE:
The Vampire's Gift

The vampire Oliver did another sort of performance for the House of Horrors. For Oliver's act, people who were very sick or very old or very sad would pay Oliver to kill them. Oliver killed them by making the people love him, love him so madly that dying seemed the only reasonable next step. He would look into their eyes and say, "My beautiful berry thicket, oh my darling marigold! We are living in a garden, full of fruit, and we eat fruit all day. We fall asleep in the sun, and when we wake, there is fruit growing from our fingertips, and we feast on each other's hands. My love, my ending, my apricot jam, you little sun-warmed wonder!" And the sick and old and sad people would lie down in Oliver's arms, who would stroke their hair until they stopped breathing.

The goat girl thought this was a vulgar sort of work. Other vampires killed people for food, or out of a predator's reflex—but Oliver killed people for kindness. Where was his animal instinct?

"Why can't you be a proper monster like the rest of us?" she asked him.

"I am not a monster at all," said the vampire Oliver. "I am an angel."

Poor freak, thought the goat girl, *he doesn't even know what he is.*

Vampires were rarely so eloquent as Oliver. Most of them spoke little and when they did speak it was usually to brag. For a species that can't look in a mirror, vampires are a vain lot. They replace the mirror with the look on a potential victim or lover's face when preening in front of them. The goat woman had to admit, she did like Oliver's way of speaking. And she liked that he wore a purple blazer with a little white turnip embroidered onto the lapel.

"The turnip is a noble root," Oliver told her over breakfast. They were sitting at long plastic banquet tables outside the fairgrounds while tent poles rose like war flags in the field. "It lives beneath the earth, bulging like a tooth. Though peppery, it does not flaunt. It would not poison you. It only lives to root and to be uprooted. It lives to serve."

"And you think this is worth emulation?" said the goat girl. "This living for servitude? What of taking what you want because you want it?"

"The turnip doesn't want anything," said Oliver.

∽

As time passed, Oliver and the goat girl became friends. For goats, there is little difference between an enemy and a friend, so it was all the same to her. Oliver was older by two or three hundred years, and he enjoyed having a younger person around. She was intelligent beyond her age, and her rectangular pupils carried a certain questioning in them that the vampire recognized as kindred. He could smell the longing she was born from like a cologne, and he could spot it in her restless motions. Vampires know yearning like they know their own names. They know that yearning can shackle you if you don't treat it kindly. So Oliver offered himself up as a sort of mentor for the child, teaching her to tend to these wants as one would a pet—and in turn, the child offered her friendship to this angel of death.

The goat girl grew and as she grew, she aged and as she aged, she learned. Oliver did not grow and he did not age, but in learning, he was just as eager. All the while, the House of Horrors wheezed down highways, puffing up like an umbrella in town after town, unsettling wealthy visitors from one coast to another. They horrified three former presidents and a host of famous painters. They disturbed an heiress' birthday party to the point of being ejected from the city limits. They performed on floating barges and in train cars, in opera houses and mansion courtyards and museum atriums. One newspaper called the House of Horrors an "*abomination*," highlighting the goat girl as "*a beast so grotesque and unladylike, women should not be permitted to purchase tickets for fear of being sullied by the monster's dreadful influence.*" Mister Pluvio had the clipping framed and hung it on the wall beside the goat girl's enclosure.

In this manner, time marched on. But eventually, Mister Pluvio grew too frail to keep up with the rigor of touring. He grew sick, and old, and sad, and one day he paid a visit to Oliver and asked Oliver to perform his act one last time. The vampire did as requested. After that, Oliver and the goat woman were free to go where they pleased.

CHAPTER SIX:
The Special Act

Behold, the special act! A domestic marvel! Watch two not-people buy a cottage by the edge of the forest! Look, ladies and gentlemen, how they behave like regular humans, cohabitating. They are washing the dishes! They are hanging laundry on the line! Hold your laughter, dear audience, hold your applause. Look, they are tilling the land, planting a garden, slicing peppers to bake into a casserole. Can you believe your eyes? These oddities, unfit for society, for any reasonable public gathering, are living like you and I! Yes, now you may laugh. Now you may laugh. The goat woman is ironing a purple jacket on an ironing board, like a proper woman. Yes, that's right, audience, she is playing house! The vampire is drinking from a glass of water and reading a book by the fire. Of course, they can never be normal. You and I know that, audience. They must keep the curtains drawn so the sunlight cannot come in. They must shoo away children who dare one another to peek in the keyholes. And of course, they can never have children of their own—thank the heavens, cross our breasts. Watch them live here in solitude, secluded from the world, in their little cabin. Watch them build lives for themselves. Gentle, strange lives.

CHAPTER SEVEN:
The Garden

Don't mistake Oliver and the goat woman for husband and wife. It wasn't like that. Anyone who loved Oliver died, of course, and the goat woman wasn't capable of loving anyway, or if she was, she had no interest in the matter. Yet together, they made a home. They were companions. They lived an easy life for the most part, but were very poor. Without the House of Horrors, neither had a way to earn a living. No shop would hire them and the age of sideshows had ended. They lived off meager savings and the few vegetables their garden would offer. Winters, when the crop was barren, troubled them. They canned turnip slices, pickled dilly beans in vinegar, preserved what little they could. But winter was long, and though the vampire could go months without eating mortal food, the goat girl was always hungry. Sometimes, her hunger overtook her like a fever, and she would thrash around the house, chewing the furniture to pieces.

One afternoon in October, a salesman came by the house. He carried a suitcase of baubles and tools—steak knives from Germany, copper buttons from Peru, a spool of red silk thread from Japanese silkworms. The suitcase unbuckled like a belt and flopped open into a showman's table, and the salesman performed an act of his own. He took one look at the goat woman and said, "I know what you need. You need a tree."

Beside the house, a large hemlock creaked.

"I already have a tree," said the goat woman. "I don't need another."

"But this tree, madam, is different! This tree, oh *this* tree, is a plum tree. Do you have any plums? Imagine, just imagine, looking out your kitchen window there and seeing forty, no fifty, no *one hundred* dark plums gleaming like garnets on the branches!"

The goat woman imagined it. As she did, a small footprint of her mother's lust kicked up in her. How the ripe plums would drop to the ground with a soft, muted thump in midsummer. How they would bleed as she sliced them to bake into sweet cakes and tarts. How the pits would crunch to dust in her jaw.

As if the salesman could read her fantasy, he spoke again.

"Ah, you misunderstand me! These plums, you mustn't eat them. They are special plums. For if you eat just one, you will long for another. And then another. And soon, a hunger so ravenous will hold you that you will not be able to stop your devouring until you have swallowed every plum on the tree, and then the tree itself, and then everything else on this earth."

"Why would you sell me a tree like that?" asked the goat woman, stunned.

"Because the tree has another power," replied the salesman. "Any other seed that is planted beneath this plum tree's shade will never stop offering a harvest, no matter the season. You will never go hungry, and never need to eat the plums, because your garden will be overrun with squash and tomatoes and cabbage and yams."

The salesman held out a closed fist. He sprung his fingers open like a ring box. In his palm was a plum pit, brittle and gray. The goat woman's stomach rumbled.

∿

After the salesman left, the goat woman planted the pit beside the vegetable garden. Oliver watched from inside the house as she dug a small hole for it with a steel spade. The goat woman waited, and tended, and in only a year's time, the pit had stretched out of the earth into a full-grown tree.

CHAPTER EIGHT:
Promises

The goat woman wasn't a fool. She knew it was only a matter of time before she ate a plum from the tree. Oliver knew this, too. As half-storied creatures themselves, they knew that no weapon this powerful could be introduced to a tale without eventually being wielded. But the goat woman was hungry, and winter would arrive soon.

"Just for a little while," the goat woman begged Oliver. "We'll let the tree grow until the garden yields enough food to last a few years. Then I'll chop it down."

"You'll never lift an axe to that tree and you know it," Oliver scoffed. "You've never killed anything in your feral little life. And you've certainly never been one for moderation."

She couldn't deny this. "Then you'll do it. If you see me eye the plums, if you catch me beginning to fall under their charm, then you take up the axe and chop down the tree yourself. I trust you to know when the time is right."

Oliver saw the hunger in his friend's eyes. He noted how skinny her wrists were, how sallow and pale her snout, how drooped her ears had grown with famine— and he thought of her plumping into health from the harvest the plum tree's shade would yield.

"All right," he said. He took the axe from the shed and he leaned it up against his bedside table, so it was near enough to grab at a moment's notice. He polished all the windows in the house so he could always peek out to monitor the tree. He stroked his friend's cheek, and kissed her forehead.

And so, the tree remained.

CHAPTER NINE:
2:00 a.m. at the Starlight Diner

"Three blueberry pancakes and a side of raw carrot stems, please."

"I'd like the steak and eggs, chérie. Keep the steak bloody."

Their waitress took the order and vanished into the kitchen.

The Starlight Diner stayed open twenty-four hours a day. Oliver and the goat woman liked to go there for breakfast long before the sun rose (for Oliver's safety) in the eastern sky. They had money now, from selling their garden's bounty of vegetables, and could afford luxuries such as a breakfast out. On this particular morning, they were debating the philosophy of their own controversial existences.

"A goat is not a monster," said Oliver, "and neither is a girl. And yet, they call you a monster. So where does this monstrousness come from? You have no monstrous gene."

The goat woman plucked a daisy from the center-piece bouquet and ate it. "Mister Pluvio was an idiot, you know. He wanted me to be all animal. He thought that renouncing my personhood is what would make me frightening. But who's afraid of a simple beast of burden?" She chewed on the petals, golden flecks catching in her teeth. "No, my monstrosity is not animal, nor human. It comes from blending the two."

The waitress arrived with both plates balanced in one hand. "Sorry, ma'am, but the chef says we can't legally serve carrot tops as food. I gave you a side of iceberg lettuce instead, hope that's all right." She placed a plate in front of each of them and zipped away to another booth.

"It's not the dark we're afraid of," the goat girl continued, "it's being in darkness with eyes that were built for the light. It's not a lone ghost we're afraid of—it's the ghost appearing in the realm of the living, in the same room as our breathing bodies. We are never afraid of a thing on its own, as it is. We're afraid of something intruding in a context in which it doesn't belong. What is a monster? It's a contradiction. A creature who houses two dissonant aspects. So yes, a girl is not monstrous on her own. Nor is a goat. But a goat is a goat and a girl is a girl, or so it should be. Nestle them side by side, in one body, and that is where the monstrosity is born. Am I a monster? Yes, love, I am. I am a monster because I contain too much." She reached across the table and laid her hoof on Oliver's hand, gently as snowfall. "What is a monster but someone who can see this world from both sides? Even you must know that. You, who live half in life, half in death. What is a monster if not someone, some thing, caught between?" She lifted a leaf of iceberg lettuce and glared at it. "The people, they want to be either here or there. Feet firmly on one shore or another. For in the middle of two shores is the sea, and the sea is unknowable, and inconstant, and cannot be controlled."

"Do you believe you are uncontrollable?" asked Oliver.

"I believe I have that potential," said the goat woman. "As did my mother."

"Your mother was but a girl, not a monster at all."

"Perhaps," said the goat woman. "But my mother believed she contained something terrible. My mother made herself into the monstress she thought she was."

"But what of this world you live in?" he replied. "Does it not contain you?"

The goat woman hesitated. "Only if I let it," she said. "Only if I leave the plums to rot."

"As you *must*," the vampire replied.

"Yes," said the goat woman. "The plums could make monsters of us all."

CHAPTER TEN:
Temptations

Did the goat woman long for the fruit? Of course she did. You would do the same. But she thought of her mother, dragged to the gallows for her passions. She thought of her father, slain for an act he did not understand. She stayed away from the tree.

All the while, the longing in her grew. She cared for it the way she would a kid. Tended it and whispered to it, cradled it to her body, let it explore under her careful watch. She fed it what scraps she could. She loved it, in her way—this wriggling want that reached for the plum tree and licked at her ribs like a flame.

"Oliver, do you think it's the goat or the girl in me that wants the plums?" she asked one evening, stirring oats in a boiling pot.

He looked up from his reading. "It's the living part," he said. "Only the living part."

CHAPTER ELEVEN:
The Men from the Village

They had been watching the goat woman. They watched her the way she watched the plums: with repulsion, with lust. They flicked their eyes over her curling horns, now bold in adulthood. They cringed at the way her soft skirts swished against her fur-bristled knees. Beyond all else they fixated on the rectangular blades of her pupils, beneath her long, elegant eyelashes. They saw an animal and they saw a lady and they trembled to see both in one seamless body. They saw how much the goat woman hungered, and it tugged them into hungering, too. "She's dangerous," they muttered to one another over their liquor. "The monster is a temptress, sent to lure us from our wives." The men fiddled with their expensive watches and tightened their silken ties. The men spied on the goat woman as she ran errands, followed her halfway home from the store again and again. "She shouldn't be so crude. She shouldn't be allowed to look at the plums that way. She shouldn't be allowed to dress like a lady if she isn't going to act like one."

People were always deciding what the goat woman was or was not allowed to want.

Listen—this next part of the story, we don't want to dwell on. It's ugly. It shouldn't have to be told. But it's important that you know it happened.

The men from the village came to the goat woman's door. Oliver was away—he'd gone to the dentist to have his teeth cleaned (vampires must maintain excellent oral hygiene). There were fourteen or fifteen men, all gathered together. Some had thrown their ties over their shoulders so as not to sully them. The only weapons they carried were their own convictions. The men from the village broke down the goat woman's door. They found her in the kitchen sautéing asparagus in butter. She only had time to turn off the stove and wipe her hooves on a dish towel before they grabbed her. *Yes, it was only a matter of time, wasn't it?* she thought. *The monsters in the stories don't get to cook asparagus. They don't get to tend their gardens. Monsters don't get to do anything, in the end, but die.* The men dragged the goat woman from her home, and through the narrow streets, and once her little home was far from view, they killed the goat woman with only their hands. Then they brought the goat woman to the butcher, who cut the goat woman into thick slices of meat, which the men seasoned and grilled and ate.

In the dentist's chair, Oliver heard a frantic drone of yearning rise up. It sounded like someone had stomped on a hornet's nest. Vampires can hear yearning up to twenty miles away, and the goat woman's was often so loud that Oliver could hardly sleep some nights from the whirring. Now it was deafening. Oliver knew something terrible had happened. He rushed through the town and he found the men reveling in their feast. The men had tossed the goat woman's head into a pile of leaves on the ground, and the head looked up at Oliver, and Oliver looked down at the head. "I'm still hungry," said the goat woman's head. "I'm hungrier than ever."

CHAPTER TWELVE:
The Plums at the End of the World

Oliver had always known that a time might come when perhaps, the world might need devouring. When the world would grow old and sad and sick, and too full of the wrong sorts of hungers. This was his art, after all. He was a master at knowing the moment when death stopped being a tragedy and became, instead, a gift. And if that time came for the whole of the world—he would be ready.

Oliver the vampire returned to the plum tree with his friend's head in his arms. Rain fell in stitches. The plums were ripe. They dragged toward the earth, so heavy were they with nectar. Oliver plucked a plum from the tree— the fattest plum, burgundy and wet with storm water. Farther off, the men dabbed grease from their chins, sleepy from their meal. In Oliver's embrace, the goat woman's head still called out. "Oliver, they've killed me, and now I have something new to yearn for. I yearn for my own yearning. They took my yearning from me."

"Hush," said the vampire, lifting the head toward the bough. "I will give you your yearning."

He stroked the goat woman's ruined fur. He pried open the jaws, already stiffening with death. And into the goat woman's mouth he placed the plum.

ACKNOWLEDGMENTS

AS ALWAYS, MY FIRST gratitude goes to my parents, Michael and Helen, and my brother, Rustin. I love you—thank you for loving me back. It's really as simple as that, isn't it?

To my friends—I'm beyond lucky to know you all. To quote one friend's mother, "It's so nice you've found these lovely people who have all the same incredibly bizarre interests as you!" I agree.

Just as loved ones helped this book be, so too did strangers. I wrote these stories while on tour with my first publication, *The Lumberjack's Dove*. Laden with a box of books, a puppet theater, and a slapdash bed crammed into the trunk of my Honda Fit, I spent eight months driving through the country with all the snake oil sales-man chic I could muster. Wake up. Drive. Perform. Sign books. Park. And then . . . write. Sometimes in my car at 2:00 a.m., parked next to a dive bar somewhere, before falling asleep in the back seat. Sometimes on a couch or in a guest room or, on one occasion, in a woodsmoke-warmed, rain-soaked yurt. No matter the city, no matter the season, I found kindness after kindness in the acquaintances and strangers who took me in. Some gave me a place to stay. Some chatted folklore and philosophy late into the night. Some showed me slivers of unfamiliar lives—which wriggled awake as new inspiration in my writing. It was their generosity that ultimately made this book possible. Thank you.

My gratitude goes to the various institutions that supported me and my work during this project: the Massachusetts Cultural Council, Vermont Studio Center, Cuttyhunk Island Writers' Residency. To all the journals that published early versions of these stories. And to the National Poetry Series and Louise Glück, who gave me my first big break back in 2017 and allowed me to start down this miraculous path.

Grand and endless appreciation for the fine folks at Vintage: production editor Kayla Overbey; copy editor Shasta Clinch; proofreaders Lyn Rosen and Lisa Davis; interior designer Christopher Zucker; cover artist Kelly Louise Judd and cover designer Mark Abrams for the dreamiest, most enchanted cover I could ask for; rock star publicist Julie Ertl; marketer Abby Endler; and my generous publisher, Suzanne Herz. And to Bobby DiTrani, who illustrated the fifty beasts within—thanks for always being down for my weird schemes.

Of course, to my fantastic agent, Paul Lucas. Your dedication and care granted me the life I've always wanted. How to repay that, I honestly don't know. Thank you.

And to Anna Kaufman, my superstar of an editor. Thank you for introducing me to Zabar's babka and the-*Titanic*-didn't-sink conspiracy theories, for always catching the Buffy allusions in my manuscripts, and for being my friend.

Last, let's give it up for my exes. If you think it's about you, it probably is. ;)

THISTLEFOOT

The Yaga siblings—Bellatine, a young woodworker, and Isaac, a wayfaring street performer and con artist—have been estranged since childhood, separated both by resentment and by wide miles of American highway. But when they learn that they are to receive an inheritance, the siblings agree to meet—only to discover that their bequest isn't land or money, but something far stranger: a sentient house on chicken legs. Thistlefoot, as the house is called, has arrived from the Yagas' ancestral home outside Kyiv—but not alone. A sinister figure known only as the Longshadow Man has tracked it to American shores, bearing with him violent secrets from the past: fiery memories that have hidden in Isaac and Bellatine's blood for generations. As the Yaga siblings embark with Thistlefoot on a final cross-country tour of their family's traveling theater show, the Longshadow Man follows in relentless pursuit, seeding destruction in his wake. Ultimately, time, magic, and legacy must collide—erupting in a powerful conflagration to determine who gets to remember the past and craft a new future. An enchanted adventure illuminated by Jewish myth and adorned with lyrical prose, *Thistlefoot* is a sweeping epic rich in Eastern European folklore: a powerful and poignant exploration of healing from multigenerational trauma told by a bold new talent.

Fiction

VINTAGE BOOKS
Available wherever books are sold.
vintagebooks.com